E. A. B. Shackleford

Virginia Dare

A Romance of the Sixteenth Century

E. A. B. Shackleford

Virginia Dare
A Romance of the Sixteenth Century

ISBN/EAN: 9783744776851

Printed in Europe, USA, Canada, Australia, Japan

Cover: Foto ©Andreas Hilbeck / pixelio.de

More available books at **www.hansebooks.com**

VIRGINIA DARE

A Romance of the Sixteenth Century

BY

E. A. B. S.,

AUTHOR OF "CECIL'S STORY OF THE DOVE," "STORIES OF
EASTER-TIDE," ETC.

NEW YORK:
THOMAS WHITTAKER
2 AND 3 BIBLE HOUSE
1892

GRATEFULLY DEDICATED TO OUR RECTOR
AND FRIEND,

Reverend Joseph Carey, D.D.,

OF

SARATOGA SPRINGS.

PREFACE.

THE author would like to remind the readers
of the romance of Virginia Dare, that if they
go back in memory to their schooldays, and the
details of their American history, they will remember that Governor White sailed for England from Roanoke on the 28th of August,
1587, leaving behind him his daughter, and her
child who had been born ten days before; that
he was unable to return immediately, owing to
war with Spain, and when after the lapse of the
three years he did return, he found the island
of Roanoke deserted, and a palisade built, as if
there had been a fight with the Indians. He
found no cross, as he had directed them to put
one if they were in trouble, over the name of
the place to which they had removed. But he
found on one tree the first three letters of the
word "Croatoan," and on another the entire
word. They attempted to find Croatoan, but,
losing their anchors, were obliged to drift away
and give up the search.

CHAPTER I.

VIRGINIA DARE:

A ROMANCE OF THE SIXTEENTH CENTURY.

CHAPTER I.

"I cannot feel
  That all is well when darkening clouds conceal
    The shining sun;
  But then I know
  God lives and loves; and say, since it is so,
    Thy will be done."

E. B. Browning.

"We've got a bright lookout, if this day is the foreteller of what our nation is to be in this new land;" and the speaker threw down his hunting-knife with a satirical laugh.

"Well, Jake, we cannot expect anything brighter if we've sense and courage enough to look before us. Ten days more and the ships will be gone; then what is there to prevent these savages from murdering us all? Our

7

colony will have a short day, and may be wiped out before it is half over. This land belongs to the redskins; and when our men and the governors fly over the water, and won't take us, it is simply saying, 'Poor things, some-one's got to stay, or the London Company won't like it: be brave, and die like Englishmen for us.'"

"What dost thou say, Hopeful Kent? Ah! thou talkest like a brave Englishman; surely, shouldst thou die as thou livest, thy country-men would have naught to be proud of in thee." Both men looked ashamed as the speaker ad-vanced from the wood, and looked straight at them with his great searching eyes, from under a broad-brimmed flat hat, such as was worn by the clergy after the Reformation.

He looked almost sternly at the two men as he asked, "Dost thou try to better things by hard work? Dost thou try to help thy gover-nor, whom thy Lord has put over thee? For shame, Jake Barnes! Didst thou work more, and growl less, thou would'st do better. Thou scarcely livest up to thy blessed calling in thy name, Hopeful Kent! How great is the mercy of thy God that he smiteth thee not!"

Jake Barnes shuffled away, muttering something to himself about "preaching parsons;" but the other man asked, "Don't you think, Master Bradford, it is rather bad luck that the day the first white baby opens its eyes in this new land should be wild and rough? I always look, sir, on the bright side when my judgment lets me, but I think it's a bad sign."

"Dost thou? See, Hopeful," cried the old man, "even now the sun has broken through. God be praised! Be there such things as thou speakest of, — chance, signs, and luck, — I wot not of them. But, even so, the day shall dawn dull and hard for us, as we have seen; but when the blessed evensong calleth, it shall be bright as yonder sky for our people, and the next day shall dawn and set with peace and plenty for them, through God's great mercy."

"A pity the first child was not a boy: we all think that, sir, don't you?"

"Ah, Hopeful, the dear Lord knoweth best! This sweet lamb of his fold, born in this heathen land, mayhap she was sent a woman that her constancy may keep her faith bright, though her way be a hard one. God bless her!"

"Why should a woman be more constant than a man, sir? I think we men make the world what it is, and it seems to me rather bad that this child is a girl. We want fighting, not constancy, now. She'll need as much care and food as if she were going to fell a dozen Indians when she's grown. There's been but little work done to-day, the men are all so excited, and all over a bit of a girl."

"There's not a man among us that knoweth the worth of a strong arm that the good Lord giveth unto his soldiers, better than I; but I have not the time to be talking to-day of the work of the blessed women in the world. It was the holy Father's will; praised be his name! Let us bow down in thanksgiving that he hath sent unto us one of his little ones; for where they go they carry his blessing. As thou art pained by the slackness among the men about the work, I'll keep thee no longer, thou may'st go to thy tasks; mayhap they will follow thy example."

"Please, Master Bradford, Mistress Wilkins sends her regards, and would have me say that she would be wanting to speak with you." The speaker was a child of ten or twelve, who courtesied as she gave her message. She was a strange-looking little figure, with her tightly plaited yellow hair drawn back from a very brown forehead. Her pale-blue eyes were a strange contrast to her skin, which was almost copper color from exposure. She wore a plain dark frock, with a kerchief neatly crossed on her breast.

The clergyman took the child's hand, saying, "I will come at once, Patience, child; art thou going back to Mistress Wilkins now?"

"Please, I will be there almost with Master Bradford, if I may first gather some of those posies to put on the cradle. Mistress Wilkins says I may rock it," said the child, looking up into the gray eyes that were smiling kindly down on her. They seemed to encourage her; for she added, clasping her hands, and fairly beaming with delight, "The baby is the most beautiful one, sir, you ever saw. I love it, oh, so much! They want to ask you about its name, and when it would please you to give it, sir."

"Ah, yes, I suppose the governor wills it to be done before we sail; sure, it must be, but I had not thought of it. He is right: I am too old for this life here; my memory is failing me. I shall go back to England and thank the blessed Lord for letting so unworthy a servant do so great a work as to receive for him two precious souls belonging to so strange a time and people, — the red savage Manteo last week; and the wee baby, the first one in a new and heathen land, this week, no doubt."

The old man had nodded his consent to the child, and walked on with bowed head, thinking aloud. The child sprang at once into a little thicket where wild vines and flowers grew in abundance, and gathered her arms full. She certainly made an odd picture; her droll little figure in that wild, unbroken country, as she stood on the branch of a fallen tree, one arm full of flowers and trailing vines, while she was trying with the other how far she could throw a flat stone and make it skip over the water. As it skipped once, twice, three times, then sank, making great circles on the smooth surface, she laughed merrily, and springing from branch to branch she ran on, jumping over every obstacle, at the same time chanting: —

> "Be thou, O God, exalted high;
> And as thy glory fills the sky,
> So let it be on earth displayed,
> Till thou art here, as there, obeyed."

It was Friday that Patience summoned Master Bradford to Mrs. Dare's hut, where only a few hours before the baby had opened its blue eyes and caused excitement in the little colony. Even Master Bradford felt a strange thrill of pleasure as Mistress Wilkins put the tiny creature into his arms, saying, "Give the child your blessing, sir: I felt it were not safe to let her be longer without at least the blessing of a priest."

As he took the little one, there was an uneasy look in his honest face. Master Bradford would not have suited some Churchmen of the present day; and yet we all look back with pride as well as pleasure to the fact that among the first colonists in this country there was a priest of our Church, and the first time that praise and worship sounded in our language from this great continent, it was in the words of our own beautiful liturgy; and thus, from Master Bradford's service in the rude Roanoke chapel, to the days of Captain John Smith, when good Mr. Hunt and Mr. Whittaker fought the strengthening Puritan element, no service had ever been offered but that of our own dear Church.

He replied, "She is the first precious lamb the Lord has trusted to this fold. 'Tis true the blessing of any of God's children is but a form of prayer to him and can do no harm."

He held many of the Puritan views that were then beginning to take root in England. It was only natural, then, that he should hesitate to comply with Mistress Wilkins's request. But he took the child tenderly, as it was laid in his arms; and as he held it and looked into its little face, so fresh from heaven, all prejudice slipped away, and he satisfied even Mistress Wilkins.

The tall figure of Governor White, and his assistant Ananias Dare, entered the room as Master Bradford began, "May our ever-loving Shepherd watch over this little lamb in this wilderness, and lead her safely through it to the heavenly fold at last. And may the blessing of the Father, the Son, and the Holy Spirit ever be with her."

It was Sunday morning, the tenth after Trinity, in the year of our Lord 1587, the 18th of August, a typical day for that time of the year, sunny and warm, with a soft haze over everything, as if the world were resting, or rather, on this particular day, in this particular place, the world looked as if it had never waked up at all. One could not believe that those lovely flowers and ferns had ever been covered with ice and snow, or that those mighty forest trees had been shaken in fierce storms till their very roots trembled in the earth. That still peaceful sheet of water, sparkling in the morning sunlight, seemed unable to lash itself into great waves, or to dash great ships into fragments.

On this little island this quiet Sunday, there was a strange sight to be seen as the drum-beat called the people to service in the little log chapel; and an odd-looking lot they were. First came two Puritan maidens, walking demurely together; then an English gentleman, whose clothes looked shabby, as did he himself; then a little company from the shore, where some canoes showed that they had just landed. Among them was a tall figure with straight black hair hanging around his shoulders: he wore a topknot of feathers, a bright blanket, an English ruff about his neck, which had been given him while he was in England; for this was Manteo, the chief who had been made a Christian only the Sunday before in this same little chapel. He had a fine figure, tall and graceful. With him came a little group of his own braves: they went straight up the hill towards the low building. Then came some slouching sailors, who looked as if they did not often go to the chapel, and were a little uncomfortable now. Then there were some men in smock-frocks. Then behind a whole family, just as you might have seen at home in England, going to any church. They were evidently people of the middle class. The father had undoubtedly been a miller before he left home, if one might judge from his funny springing step and broad miller's thumb. He looked very proud and happy as he walked along by his sturdy wife. Before them were their four children, a little rosy boy and a big girl, hand in hand, and the twins, yellow-haired English lassies. A strange mixture they all were; a little piece of civilization in the heart of a great wilderness; commonplace English people, living and worshipping in the primeval forest of the new land.

CHAPTER II.

CHAPTER II.

"Yet in sharp hours of trial
  The mighty seal must needs be prov'd:
  Dread spirits wait in stern espial: —
  But name thou still the Name belov'd."

                                        KEBLE.

THERE stood Master Bradford in gown and
bands, his kindly face upturned as he led the
prayers and psalms. He had finished reading
the lesson from St. John's Gospel, when a little
company entered the chapel and came straight
up the aisle; first Governor White's tall figure,
then Mistress Wilkins, carrying the baby, closely
followed by its father, who looked proud and
happy.

Indian and white man alike arose as Master
Bradford began the familiar and beautiful words
of our baptismal service; and when he put the
holy water on the wee brow and said, "Virginia, I baptize thee," a murmur of satisfaction
ran through the little congregation. Never was
queen baptized with more ceremony, or in the
presence of a more loving or devoted congrega-

19

tion, than this little grandchild of Governor White, who had received the name of the new country in which she was the first Christian baby born. It was because of her baptism that on this tenth Sunday after Trinity every one in the little Roanoke colony but the child's own mother crowded into and around the roughly made log building that served for a church or chapel.

That first house of God in our land, which now, three hundred years later, abounds in splendid churches and cathedrals, was, I fancy, as precious to him who values our gifts by our love, and counts worth by sacrifice, as the gorgeous temples of our day. He did not despise the roughly made house in which the Holy Presence was first celebrated; that log room where there was moss for a carpet, a great bowlder for the altar, lichen and cup-moss for hangings, the font, a spring trickling through the stones; where for decorations the sweetbrier and wild creeper had forced their way between the logs, and clung to the barky walls, and where the little birds often flew in for their morning hymn of praise, and the forest trees raised their arms protectingly over the holy spot, forming, as it were, a lofty cathedral arch. To those loving Eyes watching from above, that

humble square building, made by the loving
hands of those first settlers as a token of their
love and gratitude for bringing them safely
through the mighty waters to so pleasant a port,
that first chapel, I am sure, was as beautiful as
are many of our richly carved and polished
temples of stone.

As the service ended, the little congregation
gathered outside the governor's hut; inside,
some of the principal men were talking to him,
also Manteo, the Indian chief. Governor White
was standing in the inner room by the bed; he
was holding the baby in his arms, and speaking
very earnestly. A voice from the bed cried,
" O father, father dear, you will not leave me!
do not, do not."

" Yes, Eleanor," was the reply; " God calls
me back to England. I only waited to see your
baby; with her you will find it less lonely, dear,
and you are always brave." And, as Ananias
Dare came in and bent over the bed, Governor
White walked out to the group of men waiting
in the outer room. He closed the door behind
him as he said, " Well, my men, I think this is
a good time and place for me to tell you the
plans we are to carry out."

And then, stepping to the door, that those

standing outside might hear what he said, he continued, "This is our plan: I shall sail for England as soon as we can make everything ready. Some of the men will go with me, the others remain here till our return. I do not mean in this particular place, but in this wonderful new country. I do not think it would be wise to remain on this island; any of the tribes which wish to drive you away have the advantage, being able to approach you on every side in their canoes. You are to leave Roanoke and go to the mainland, and settle in a spot not held by any particular tribe. Wanchese is no longer friendly; partly, I believe, because he thinks that at one time this island belonged to his tribe. However this may be, I am assured that it would be better for you to be on the mainland for many reasons, and that it would be wise for you to have nothing to do with Wanchese. When you leave Roanoke, carve on a tree that overhangs the little bay the name of the place you have removed to; if in danger or distress, carve over the name a cross. I have drawn up the laws that are to govern you, and which will be in my room ready for you to sign to-morrow. I will leave behind me ninety-one men, the seventeen women, and eight children, and these laws are to govern them."

As the governor saw the dissatisfied faces, he continued, "I shall return as soon as it is possible: I am sure you cannot doubt that. Am I not leaving you good security, my daughter and her child, this dear little one?"

He laid his hand on the swinging cradle in which he had put the baby; and then, raising the other hand and looking up, he said in a clear, distinct, and reverent way, "Before you all, my friends, and before my God, I swear I will be faithful to you. I will do to you as I hope and pray I may be done by. I shall remember you, as I want you to remember my laws and wishes, for which we shall have to answer in the day of the great Judgment."

The men outside shuffled off, while those inside who belonged to the council talked long with the governor. Manteo listened, and admired the white chief's power and wisdom.

The next day the men, though they had made many threats, one by one signed the laws that were to govern the colony.

Then there came days of busy preparation for the return of the ships to England, and the comfort of those to be left behind. Another baby face appeared, and the happy family of children now numbered five. Mr. Harvey proudly

brought his baby to Master Bradford to receive
its name, — Elizabeth.

Then came the dreadful day when the ships
weighed anchor and passed out of sight, lost forever to those who watched their departure.

When Governor White's return to England
was talked of, the colonists dreaded the time of
his leaving; they shrank from even thinking of
it, and yet they did not begin to know what his
departure meant to them.   A handful of people
in a great land among savages.

Mrs. Dare grew strong very slowly; had it not
been for her baby, it is doubtful whether she
ever would have rallied after parting with her
father and husband; but that tiny face was a
precious treasure, not only to the mother who
watched it so lovingly, but also to every one in
that little colony.   There were few men, even,
who did not look in at the door of the little hut
some time in the course of every day " to take a
look at the baby."   She would allow herself to
be picked up by any one, at any time, without
a murmur; in fact, the only time she had ever
really cried, and then she did it with all her
might, was while the governor's ships were
weighing anchor and slowly moving out of sight.
Mistress Wilkins said the child was troubled

with colic, but there were others who shook their heads and talked about omens and children's wonderful power of foreseeing dangers or calamities while they were too young to talk, save with angels or spirits. But, be the case what it may, the fact remains that Virginia was an exceptionally good baby, did not cry at all till she was ten days old, and never again to amount to anything. This is perhaps why baby Elizabeth Harvey was not more loved; she was from the first a delicate child, and had more than her share of baby ailments and pains, and she was always crying, or just ready to begin at the slightest provocation. Some people were unkind enough to say that her mother deserved to have such a child, for calling her after the queen; that she would have just such a temper when she was grown up; while Virginia would be placid, sweet, and sunny, like the land of her name and birth.

Virginia was nearly five weeks old when the first change came into her baby life; in fact, this change was destined to affect the whole colony.

CHAPTER III.

CHAPTER III.

" Lay hands unto this work with all thy wit,
Yet pray that God may speed and profit it."
ROBERT SALTERNE.

IT was the very last of September; the day
had been a perfect one, just the faintest touch
of autumn in the air and on the trees. The
sun had gone down in a sea of glory, and the
peaceful hour of twilight was hushing everything to rest. The sentinel was pacing to and
fro. It was Jake Barnes's turn that night, and
he did not like the work at all; in fact, it was
hard to find anything in the way of work that
he did like.

As he came to a sudden halt by an old tree
that overhung the water he muttered, " It's lots
of good I'd do if the redskins should come ! I
suppose they'd like me to kill 'em all. A nice
lot of cowards the fellows here are ; why don't
they go and fight them savages, and let us take
their lands to pay us for coming away across the
water; frighten them, let 'em see we mean busi-

ness. If we don't, they'll finish us all. I wouldn't make friends with any of 'em; carrying them around the world as if they were white Christians; and just because they call one a chief, he must be treated like a king. I hope some day I'll have the pleasure of putting my sword through that red shining-faced Manteo."

He stopped suddenly, for a slight sound on the bank below caught his ear. He stepped quickly behind the tree, so that if there were an arrow coming it could not possibly touch his precious body. As none came, he gathered all his courage and called out, "Who goes there?"

Immediately a soft voice answered, "Don't fire, Master Barnes! It's only me, Patience."

"What are you doing there? You deserve to be shot," was the gruff reply.

"Oh, please don't!" cried Patience. "I was only watching the stars come out to look in their looking-glass. Do you know, Master Barnes, that the sea is the looking-glass for the sun and moon and all the little stars? To-night the moon-mother has stayed at home, but she has sent some clouds to take care of her star-children, and as soon as they look at themselves for a little while, their nurses, the clouds, carry them away home. Pretty soon they'll be all gone, and then the sky will be lonely."

Barnes walked on, and had forgotten the child. Passing the same spot a few minutes later, he started at the sound of a soft voice saying, "Master Barnes!" Patience stood beside him; the hand she had laid on his sleeve shook, and her upturned face was very white, while she said in a voice that trembled with fear, "There is a canoe coming over from the land, and there's an Indian in it, I think."

"Where, child? Are you sure?"

"Oh, yes," she replied; "and I was so frightened I hurried to find you."

"I'll make short work of him if he's alone, I will," Barnes muttered. "One of Manteo's fine braves, I hope. I wish it were the old fellow himself, I'd soon put a ball through his royal crown, and not feel bad about it either;" and he laughed to himself. Then, turning to Patience, he said, "Where is he coming ashore?"

"He was pointing towards the little bay, Master Barnes; but," she added, "if he's one of Manteo's Indians, we ought not to hurt him, ought we?"

"You go to bed, child, and mind you say

nothing of this; it's my duty to shoot any one
that's lurking around in a suspicious way; I
ought to have shot you. I'll have to do it now,
if you don't hurry to bed and go to sleep. Off
with you! I guess your Indian was all a
fancy."

Patience waited for nothing more: she almost
flew toward the little group of cabins, until she
was hidden from Barnes by the woods. Then,
with an anxious look behind, to see he was not
following her, she stood still. Barnes had no
idea of following her; he watched her out of
sight, descended the bank to a rock from which
he could command a good view of the little bay,
and sat down, ready to fire.

Meanwhile, Patience stood in the old forest
alone. As her feet had been flying over the
ground, her mind had been flying too. In less
than half the time it takes to write it, she
thought over what Barnes had said about killing
one of Manteo's men; she also remembered what
she had heard Mrs. Dare say one day, after
Manteo had been in to see the baby Virginia,
"Manteo is a faithful friend to us. If the Indians ever give us trouble he will stand by us to
the very end." Perhaps this was one of his
men; perhaps he was bringing a message from

Manteo; perhaps it might be Manteo himself. Some one must save him.

Before she could reach the huts to call any one, the canoe would reach the bay; she was the one to save him. But what if Master Barnes should see her and shoot her! For one moment the thought frightened her, and she crouched down on the ground. Another, and the brave resolution was made. She must save the man in the canoe. Once more she was flying through the dark forest.

Well for the baby Virginia, and for all in that little colony, that her steps were light and quick, and her heart was brave.

Patience reached the clearing on the ridge of the bank; on she moved stealthily, one slip and she would be in that dark, cruel water. Well for her work that the clouds had hidden all the stars. She came to the group of rocks standing out in the water; at the same moment she heard the soft splash of the paddle. One quick spring and she reached the first slippery stone. Could she stand firmly enough to jump to the next rock? If not, within a few seconds the canoe would have passed beyond her reach. The paddle sounded nearer; how her head whirled; what a giddy spring! But it was done.

" Chief Manteo ! "

The paddle stopped; she repeated her words; the canoe came closer. " Who are you?" she asked.

The Indian took her hand and felt it, as if to try to understand who or what she was, then he replied in broken English, " Ranteo comes from Manteo to the white chief. Why is the white child here alone on the rocks?"

" I came here to save you, for you must not go into the little bay. Master Barnes will not know who you are. He says it is his duty to shoot every one that is about at this hour."

The Indian muttered something in his own tongue that was hardly complimentary to the whites. While Patience was trying to get up her courage to make the difficult spring back toward the land, the canoe had been concealed under some bushes, for Ranteo did not feel quite sure the whites were to be trusted; if so, why should this child come to warn him? He thought of all this as he drew his canoe up on land and hid it. He was standing, holding his hand out to Patience before she had gained courage enough to move. She took his hand and tried to jump, but the fright that had lent her strength was over now, and she was trembling and unsteady. Ranteo drew her to the rock on which he stood, then, raising her to his shoulder, stepped across to the land. He did not put her down, but turned into the unbroken forest by a path or trail which his Indian eye had traced.

CHAPTER IV.

CHAPTER IV.

"Little by little, sure and slow,
We fashion our future, of bliss or woe,
    As the present passes away.
Our feet are climbing the stairway bright,
Or gliding downward into the night,
    Little by little, day by day."

IN less than ten minutes they were passing
the first log hut; how quiet everything was!
Most of the settlers were sleeping as sweetly as
they might have done in their own villages in
dear old England.   There was not much doubt
which of the huts was occupied by the Harvey
family, for the baby Elizabeth was crying as
usual.   No one seemed to trouble himself in the
least about the wee creature that sent forth con-
stantly so pitiful a little cry, that it said more
plainly than volumes could have done, how
weary and hard she found this world.

She, the youngest creature, was the first to
break the peace of that quiet little Roanoke village, the first Christian people in this heathen
land.   But the happy hours of peace in their

rude little homes were over; for in less than an
hour every one's heart echoed the sad cry of that
tiny baby: there were torches lighted here and
there, and little knots of men talking in anxious
whispers, as if they feared being overheard, even
by the wind and trees; women standing together
outside their doors, with frightened children
clinging to them. Every one was thoroughly
awake now. In one group stood Anthony Gage,
an elderly man who seemed to have authority,
for the others were looking at him and listening.
He had been made a leader rather by circum-
stances than by birth; and he looked frightened
and bewildered now, as the torch cast a lurid,
flickering light over his handsome face.

"I think," he was saying, "as long as Manteo
is a powerful chief, we had better go back with
Ranteo; we will be as safe there as anywhere.
It was certainly good of him to offer us shelter,
for it will mean war with Wanchese for him.
What say you, men?"

Hopeful Kent was in the group, and spoke up
at once: —

"I fear we shall then be making slaves of ourselves. Manteo can do what he likes with us
when we are in his camp. Mayhap he has made
all this story up to get possession of us."

The first speaker shook his head. "No," he said, "Manteo is our friend; an Indian is not treacherous to his friends. I have feared, ever since Governor White left us, that we should have trouble with Wanchese; for if an Indian is not one's friend, he is his bitter enemy. I wish we could have removed our village at once. The delay was unavoidable, as you all know."

Gage had one of those weak natures, to which it is almost impossible to form a positive and quick decision. As he paced up and down at a short distance from the others, the group was joined by several persons, among whom was Barnes, more put out than he chose to acknowledge at the turn things had taken. He had had no opportunity to fire on the Indian as he had planned, and then, worst of all, a redskin had got the best of him. Altogether, he was in a much worse humor than usual, if that were possible.

Why did such unwholesome, unprincipled men come away from their own land, where the laws could hold them in check?

Barnes was saying in a strong, fierce way, "I tell you what it is, lads, it's each man for himself. We haven't any one over us. I, for one,

sha'n't put my red scalp in the keeping of any
Indian. I'd be for taking the one that has come
here and quartering him, and sending a piece to
his fine painted chief, and the rest to Wanchese.
It'll make peace with him quicker than anything
else we can do."

The tall governor, Gage, had been absent
hardly five minutes from the group, when he returned, still undecided, to find the aspect of
things totally changed.

He began mildly, "I think, my dear fellows,
we had better get our things together, and start
at daybreak. Ranteo will wait, I have no doubt."

A growl rather than a murmur ran through
the little group; then Barnes spoke out: —

"We're not going, sir, one step with that ras-
cal. He can wait till we scalp him; it's all he
deserves; stealing in among us like a thief in
the night. We are going to be men, and fight
for our homes, our women, and children; aren't
we, lads?"

"Ay, ay," was the reply. But one strong
voice, from a man scarcely more than a lad, who
had just come up, said, "Do you call yourselves
men? It is cowards I should call you if you
would touch one who has come among us to
save us from ruin, and who trusts us. For shame,

fellows! If you touch him, it must be over my dead body."

"I shouldn't mind that at all," said Barnes dryly, drawing out his hunting-knife.

George Howe, for such was the name of the speaker, was no coward; but he realized that this was not the time for a quarrel among themselves, when trouble and death threatened from outside. So he only said, "Put up your knife, Barnes; if we kill each other, there will be one man less, if not two, to guard the women and children. I am sure you would be sorry to see this brave fellow killed. If Wanchese should come, and you find all he tells us is true, Governor White would be very angry if we should hurt an Indian without good cause."

"I care much about his anger, or what he wishes," grumbled Barnes; while Hopeful Kent muttered, "I'm mighty sure the governor will never be bothered with our doings; there will be none left to tell him. We'll all be in Kingdom Come long before he or any one else comes back. It's a lot any of them trouble themselves about us." Once more Howe tried to thwart the evil councils of the lawless men among whom he stood.

"Let's put it to vote what we shall do,"

Barnes said, coming up to the group, after he had interviewed a number of the men, who still stood in little knots talking anxiously. Howe and the present governor, Gage, were standing together a little apart. Howe had made a suggestion, and had almost succeeded in persuading his companion to adopt it, when Barnes cried out in triumphant tones, "Let's put it to vote, we are free men."

"If you let them," muttered Howe, "it will be the ruin of us all, sir; something, it must be the Evil One, I think, gives Barnes a strange power over the men. Don't put it to vote, sir, I beg; make them feel your authority."

"No doubt you are right, Howe," replied Gage, as he stepped nearer to Barnes and said, "Barnes, you have the interest of us all at heart, and while I feel it is right to observe caution, in this case we have no choice but to trust Manteo. Were we alone we might run risks, which we have no right to do with the women and children depending on us. I know you will trust my decision, which I am sorry to say differs from your opinion." He stopped, for Barnes had turned and walked away. He only went a few steps, however; then turning with a gleam of triumph in his eyes, as he saw the disturbed look he had caused in the face of the man whom he ought to have obeyed, he cried furiously, " Don't be too sure of your good judgment; we came to this country free men, and as a free man I am going to act now. I am not going to Croatoan. You may if you choose. Who'll fight the savages, and win lands and homes with me? or run away like a baby to its mother when the first sound of fight comes."

Nearly all the men had gathered round, seeing their leader standing in a weak, undecided way, looking helplessly and distractedly at Barnes, whose strong, magnetic face they all felt; and they cried, almost with one voice, " I, Barnes, I ! I am no coward." " I am an English lad," or " Here's your man, Barnes." Seeing that he held the men, he stepped before the tall figure of Anthony Gage, who had authority and power at that moment had he only had the strength to exert it, and began, " If we are agreed to stay here and fight like men, the first thing we can do to prove the strength of our resolution is to act upon it; to put to death this lying Indian who has come among us to be a spy, to make trouble, to get possession of us and our women and children, to torture us, to put us to death. Do you not say with me that he should be punished, to show those red dogs we mean real work, and no more fooling? What do you say, fellows?"

Only a few voices replied; even they assented feebly. Howe walked away in disgust. Barnes, feeling a little uncertain as to the wisdom of his last suggestion, determined to excite his followers a little more before Ranteo should be spoken of again. So he continued, "The red villains will be on our track by morning, as soon as they find their comrade doesn't come back, so we must get to work and build a palisade. If they once get hold of us they will show no mercy, though some of you are foolish enough to be afraid of hurting this precious copper-colored heathen. I confess I am not womanish enough for that."

More than a score of voices cried out, "Nor I, nor I." "They are an ungodly lot." "Clear them off the face of the earth; it's a Christian man's duty." Gage stood with bowed head, the very personification of disgust, yet with not moral courage enough to right the wrong he was so horrified at. He had tried to be a good man, and yet please his fellow-men among whom he was thrown; strange to say, an aim which is seldom realized, even when a whole life is given to its accomplishment. The most truly popular lives are apart from, and without thought of, self; lived for one's fellow-men, with a brighter and more perfect mainspring than mere humanitarianism. Such lives become more than good, and without either knowing or realizing it, the busy, flippant world stops in its rush to admire, if not to bow down in adoration.

When Howe left the little company, he walked carelessly away, but only while in sight did he go with slow steps and bowed head. Once out of sight, and sure he was not watched, he ran as fast as he could under the shadow of the trees. Going behind each hut, he looked inquiringly at the inmates, but he reached the very end before he felt satisfied.

It was indeed a pretty sight he saw there; the rude room with its few articles of rough furniture, and a few little decorations which gave the place a refined, home-like air; at one side swung a cradle, in which lay the baby Virginia. By the cradle stood the beautiful young mother, looking proudly and lovingly down on her child. The rush torch which she held threw a bright light on the little creature, on the mother herself, and on a tall figure that knelt by, watching the child with almost reverent awe, only ventur-

ing to touch the tiny hand with the tip of his
long finger. The baby watched him with her
pretty blue eyes, cooing as the long feathers
waved back and forth as he moved his head.

"The child comes from the Great Spirit," the
Indian said.

Mrs. Dare replied quietly, "Truly, Ranteo,
the Great Spirit sent her. She is his, but he
has given her to us for a while. You will be
her friend always, won't you? If anything
should happen to me, I tremble to think what
would become of my baby."

Ranteo did not speak, but he took the baby's
wee hand and laid it against his forehead, then
pressed it to his lips, and made a vow which he
never forgot. Nor did he forget those words,
"She is His."

Howe had been weighing several plans in his
mind. At last he was resolved, and stepped in,
saying, "Ranteo, come with me."

"Ranteo's work will be to carry the white
lady and the Great Spirit's baby to Manteo's
wigwam," was the reply.

"Thank you, Ranteo, we will be very glad to
have you, both baby and I," Mrs. Dare said in
her sweet way; but glancing at Howe's face she
stopped suddenly and asked, "What is wrong,
do tell me."

"I might as well," replied Howe. "Barnes has made himself governor, and decrees that all Indians shall die, and the white men shall not go to Croatoan."

Mrs. Dare clasped her hands in horror, but the Indian showed no sign of surprise or fear, and Howe continued, "There is no time to lose; come, Ranteo, and don't lay up all these shameful things against our whole race."

Without a word, Ranteo took from his belt the small soft skin of a white rabbit, and laid it on the cradle, then followed Howe. Long before Barnes and his men had finished their discussion, Ranteo had slipped off in the stillness of the night, wondering in a stupid sort of a way why white men were so unlike each other, that a child had risked her life to save him from being shot when carrying a warning of danger and an offer of hospitality, and that after delivering both, his life was still so unsafe that he had to be smuggled away quietly. As his canoe glided quietly over the dark water, he was glad the pale-faces were far behind, but he wished that sweet, blue-eyed papoose had a red skin.

After seeing Ranteo's canoe safely out of sight, Howe turned back toward the line of moving torches, which showed where the huts were. As he saw them moving he decided the council must be over, and work of some kind begun. "God only knows what those villains will be up to next. Barnes hates me. It will be better for him 'not to know that I had anything to do with Ranteo's escape. I'm sure he wouldn't mind taking me in his place, and I shall be needed by the women and children. It's little consideration they'll have while that brute is self-imposed governor of the colony," he said as he hurried on.

Mrs. Dare was holding the baby, and she looked up as he entered. "Did he get off, Howe?" she asked.

"Yes; he's far across the water by this time, and the villains are just beginning to look for him. I fancy I see the torches coming this way," he replied.

"Thank God," she said; "it would have been a disgrace to our people. Oh, if my father were only here! What is to become of us all?"

"You will hear soon enough," was the reply. "Here comes our gallant new governor; it is best to be ignorant about Ranteo."

CHAPTER V.

CHAPTER V.

" Oh, the little birds sang east, and the little birds sang west,
    And I said in an underbreath,
    All our life is mixed with death
    And who knoweth which is best?"

                  BROWNING.

HOWE had hardly finished speaking when the light of another torch flashed through the doorway, and with it appeared Barnes's ugly face, with his red hair standing straight up, literally on end, as it always was, giving him the appearance of being in a chronic state of fright; but unless his own hideous nature frightened him, which I am afraid he had not grace enough to see as it really was, his appearance must have been merely a reflection of the contorted, misshappen soul within.

Eleanor Dare was one of a fine old English family who nearly all had served their country with their swords, on land or sea. She had all the elements of a soldier; was a brave, noble woman. Her figure, which was slight and graceful, to Barnes looked strangely tall and commanding as she rose and came to meet him, still holding her baby.

"What do you want? and who are you that you make yourself a ruler?"

Though Barnes boasted of fearing neither God nor man, there was something very cowardly in his nature: it made him shrink back now before the eyes of this brave woman, who dared to stand alone and accuse him of what he had done.

"You have not heard the truth, madam," he said, almost civilly: "some one has been telling you lies; it is the men who have said what we shall do."

In a gentler tone she said, "If that is really the case, I will apologize. Without doubt you have sent some little gift to Manteo as a token of our gratitude?"

"Sent! why we hoped to find the messenger here. We were just about to prepare a gift for the chief. The men think it better not to go to Croatoan; we are going to make all quite safe here. But," he added, "the Indian is not here, is he?"

"Here? oh, no. Mistress Wilkins is sleeping in the back, and Howe was talking to me here. Was it Ranteo who brought the message?"

And Barnes, seeing her great blue eyes, and

knowing little of a woman's power to act a part perfectly when something great is involved, never guessed she was deceiving him, as he replied, " Yes, it was Ranteo, I think."

" Did you tell him to wait, that you wanted to send a present to Manteo?" she asked.

" No; I didn't think of it," Barnes muttered as he turned away. When he had reached his men, who stood a little way off, he continued, " I am afraid if I had told him what the present was to be, he wouldn't have been any more anxious to wait. But I'll tell you what it is, fellows, they haven't seen him, they don't know anything about him. Folks can't fool me. The red scoundrel must have heard something we said, and skipped; like enough he'll bring his whole tribe back here to scalp us all by morning."

It was well for the little stars that their cloud nurses carried them off to bed early; for I am sure they would have felt very sad had they watched the changes fast appearing in the quiet little village of Roanoke, through the long hours of that September night. The night heron saw it all, and sent forth its mournful wail of sorrow. But at last there was a lurid line of red along the eastern horizon, the dark sky was shot with streaks of crimson, and the day broke softly.

The sun peeped down on the English colony, and found it wholly different from the place she had left twelve hours before. The row of log huts stood empty and deserted, many of them had lost their roofs or sides, wherever there were strong logs they had been removed; there were no signs of waking life about the place; everything was desolate. A few things were strewn around, showing the haste of the departure. At the lower end of the island some trees were hewn down, and just beyond rose a palisade made of large timbers; behind it, all the settlers were gathered in a confused crowd. The children were crying or fretful; the women worn out and weary; most of the men thoroughly out of temper, many of them swearing against Manteo for having, as they said, disturbed their peaceful lives, or against Queen Elizabeth for having sent them away to die alone, like the children of Israel in the wilderness.

The day wore on as it had first dawned, clear and bright, but with a decided chill in the air, which by night threatened almost a frost. The women and children who were exposed felt it keenly; and the little ones joined Elizabeth Harvey's sad wail, all but Virginia, who lay peacefully looking up at the blue sky and the fleecy

clouds; her great blue eyes seemed to understand what all the confusion meant, and she
uttered not a murmur.

When darkness crept over the land once more,
bringing with it a penetrating coldness, the men
threw themselves on the ground with whatever
covering they could find, and went to sleep.
Many of the children cried themselves to sleep,
and most of the tired women soon followed
them. Only in one corner a little group was
still awake; on the ground where the bushes
formed a rude shelter lay Mrs. Harvey. She
had been about very little since the baby came.
The exertion and excitement of the move had
proved too much for her. Mistress Wilkins was
caring for her as best she could, without the aid
of medicine, or even comforts, while Mrs. Dare
tried to soothe poor little Elizabeth. Harvey sat
by, looking sadly at his wife, and with each
weary breath she drew his heart grew more
heavy, and a greater sense of desolation crept
over him. The watchers watched on in silence;
all was still save the cry of the heron or the
screech of the owl in the forest, when a low
whistle sounded from the northern end of the
palisade, followed by a flash of light from a
torch which was held one moment high in the

air. This was to be Howe's signal of danger, for he was stationed that night. Harvey sprang to his feet and began waking the sleeping men. Barnes had only half opened his eyes, when a hideous war-cry sounded through the forest. In an instant every man was on his feet, with his hand on his rifle, ready for the fight. Then came the arrows thick and fast; from the inside of the palisade the guns boomed, or a sword clashed against the Indian who tried to mount the palisade. The redman's war-whoop sounded on every side, now and then a flash of lightning, for a storm was gathering, showed the hideous paint on their copper-colored faces. The noise woke the birds from their sleep, and drawing their little heads from under their wings they sent forth doleful cries to add to the horror of the scene. Even the leaves seemed to sigh with grief at the awful sight.

Patience had crouched close to Mrs. Dare, and was helping her to soothe the babies, when she asked, " If the Indians get us all, what will they do with us?"

Mrs. Dare held her baby more tightly as she replied, " Patience, even if they are savages, they are under the power of our God whom they do not know, and he can take care of us if the Indians do break through the palisade; they can do nothing without his knowing it. You and I cannot fight, dear, but we can pray."

Patience sat a few moments silent before she spoke again. "Do you know," she said, "I don't feel afraid, that is, very much afraid, for the stars have just come through the clouds; though there are only two or three, they are watching us, and they are so sorry; they are blinking very hard to keep their tears back. See how they blink and twinkle. I know they are angels' eyes."

A sudden wild yell in the forest sent terror to every heart. The men had all they could do to keep back Wanchese and his braves. Several of the settlers had been already wounded, and one killed. They could not hold out much longer against their present enemy, and if help had come to Wanchese they were surely lost. Only one moment did this thought depress them, for the instant the savages heard the cry, they sent up one fierce and wild answer, and turned to meet the new foe, now rushing upon them, headed by Manteo.

Then the Englishmen fired a fresh volley, helping Manteo to drive Wanchese rapidly back to the shore. The fight was over for the time, just

as morning dawned. Ranteo, with three other
Indians, all in paint and war toggery, were
standing without the palisade. Howe went to
see what they wanted. All expected only a
command to surrender, and become Manteo's
prisoners. But no, Ranteo only handed Howe
a soft, well-cured deerskin, saying, "Manteo
sends Ranteo to take the skin to the Blue-eyes,
and will the Blue-eyes and the beautiful lady go
with Ranteo to Manteo's wigwam?"

He would not come inside the palisade, and
Howe was not very anxious to have him, as he
felt he could not trust Barnes. But he took the
skin and message to Mrs. Dare.

As she listened, her eyes filled with tears, and
she said, "How noble and good of Maneto!
But I will not leave the others. Can we not all
go now? Surely this dreadful night is enough."

Howe shook his head. "Those Indian bodies
outside craze the men. Nothing will satisfy
them now. Many of them would go through
anything in the world to shoot an Indian again.
But go with your baby; you will be safer there
than here," he said.

"No," she replied firmly; "I will stay with
my people to the last. Thank him for me,
Howe, and tell him what I say."

Howe gave the message, and Ranteo went away disappointed.

Hopeful Kent took very good care to keep in as safe a place as possible during the fight, yet he had an arrow wound in his left arm. Mrs. Dare had bathed it, and was binding it up for him, when Patience ran up and said, "Mistress Wilkins wanted her in a hurry, please." She went quickly to the elder-bush which sheltered the place where Mrs. Harvey lay. She had roused enough to take her poor baby. Mistress Wilkins was bending over her; just as Eleanor Dare came up, she opened her eyes and looked around as if to find some one. Then her lips moved, and they could just hear her say, "Martin!" He heard her, and was by her side in a second. But the lips had closed forever.

The baby stirred and began its mournful wail, as Eleanor lifted it gently out of the mother's arms, where it would never lie again. The morning sun sent down a long golden ray, which forced its way through the trees, and lighted the pale face that was at rest forever. The whole forest, birds and animals, seemed to wake to life together, and began their hymn of praise and thanksgiving just as Mistress Wilkins crossed the hands on the still breast, saying,

" Grant her eternal rest, O Lord, and may perpetual light shine upon her! "

Mrs. Harvey's death was one more horror added to that awful night. All seemed too much stunned by what they had been through, to be shocked, or even much surprised, at anything. Howe helped poor Martin Harvey to make a rude coffin, in which they laid the body of Elizabeth's mother. Patience gathered vines and flowers, and laid them about the peaceful face. At sunset the deposed Governor Gage read the service, and they carried the coffin away. The twins, poor little things, cried bitterly, as did the little rosy boy, and the big girl, who tried hard to take her mother's place to the other three. And the poor baby, Elizabeth, wailed more sadly than ever.

Another night crept on, and the summer seemed to have come back for a little while. Though it was warm, not one star came out, and Patience was afraid. Once more the dreadful yell, once more the forest was alive with Wanchese's men. Fierce and wild was the fight between the red and the white men. Here and there the palisade began to yield; a blazing arrow had set more than one place on fire. Cries and yells again made the night hideous. The owls and herons once more joined in with their weird, screeching cry.

Mrs. Dare sat holding the two babies, the women and children were huddled about her, when Howe called her away out of their hearing.

"An hour more and the palisade must fall. you must not be here then. You had better go to Maneto quickly."

"How can we?" she asked simply.

"I have a plan," he said. "It is dangerous, but it is more dangerous for you to stay here; every moment makes the place less safe."

CHAPTER VI.

CHAPTER VI.

"Many are pains of life, I need not stay to count them; there is no one but hath felt some of them, though unequally they fall." — UGO BASSI'S SERMON.

SCARCELY ten minutes had passed before the group of women and children stood by a little opening which Howe had made in the palisade, through which they were to escape into the forest. Howe stepped out first. Why should the leaves rustle so? He fancied he heard a noise near. An arrow might pierce him in a second, or one of those frightful yells might announce their discovery.

But no arrow came, and one by one the little procession filed out behind him into the dark forest. It was by no means easy work to keep on. The underbrush crackled and scratched the children's hands and feet until they cried and had to be hushed. Only the baby Elizabeth would not be silenced, though Mrs. Dare did all she could to soothe her.

"They will certainly hear her and find us.

67

We'll be all scalped if you carry her any farther," said one of the women.

But Mrs. Dare's answer silenced her. "If either of the children is making noise enough to endanger you all, we ought not to remain together. I will keep behind till you are all safe."

Mistress Wilkins was just behind, carrying little Martin Harvey. He was a stout child, really too heavy a load for the poor old woman, yet she had energy enough left to turn savagely on the first speaker. "You ought to be a heathen savage with a red skin," she said, "to talk of leaving a poor motherless baby alone in the woods for the wild beasts. I wonder the Lord don't send some of them out to tear you to pieces. You are no Christian woman."

On, on they went, groping their way through the darkness, often stumbling, sometimes falling, but keeping on bravely, carrying the children, and helping the more frightened ones. Suddenly they came to a clearing, and before them stretched the great ocean. They all gathered close together under the old trees that shaded even the very edge of the bank. Then Howe told them he must leave them while he went to bring the boats. Most of the women began to cry, saying they surely would be killed without a man to protect them, until Eleanor Dare said, in her quiet, decided way, "Go, Howe, we are quite safe here among the trees and bushes. The great danger will be when we are on the water."

"You had better not talk, or even move; and be sure you do not answer any call, or speak to any one, until the signal of a low whistle is given," Howe said warningly, as he disappeared into the forest.

It seemed a century since he left them; it was in fact only about thirty minutes before they heard his whistle, and he appeared carrying an end of one of the boats. Harvey was carrying the other end, and behind them came two men carrying another. Hopeful Kent was one, and he was grumbling about the weight.

The boats were soon launched, the women were getting in, Howe was lifting in the little ones, when suddenly Hopeful Kent sprang into the nearest boat and pushed it from the shore. "What are you doing?" cried a dozen voices. He only pushed the harder, muttering, "I hear the red scoundrels coming." He was mistaken, however: no one came, but they could not persuade him to come back. He said he had as big a load as he was going to row, and was soon out of sight.

"I dare not put another one in," Harvey said to Howe, as the small boat dipped to the water's edge. Mrs. Dare, who had refused to get in till all were settled, still stood holding the two babies, and by her Patience and Mistress Wilkins. Howe looked at them helplessly for a moment, then suddenly exclaimed, "I have an idea, Harvey! you and Thompson see this boat safely to Croatoan. Tell them Mrs. Dare is coming, and that it will be all right. If we do not come, you had better come back and take the rest of the men. I am going to try to steal two of the canoes, if I am seen and caught, they will have to wait for you; be sure you come back." The two men clasped hands for a moment, and the boat slipped silently over the still water. Howe told Mrs. Dare his plan ; leaving his hat, shoes, and whatever else he did not need, he scrambled along the bank just over the water. Very soon he could see the palisade, and the torch-light showed the Indians' ugly faces. He remembered Governor White's directions about the name of the place they should remove to, and as he reached the edge of the little bay, he drew himself up to a tree, and taking out his knife began to carve the word CRO-ATO-AN; but only three letters were done when he noticed a commotion among the Indians, and fearing to be seen, he slipped down into the water. It was strange that the Indians had left the canoes unguarded, but they looked upon the pale-faces as a stupid race, and they felt so sure that they were all enclosed behind the palisade, they had left only one man to watch the boats. He was more interested in the fight than in his duty, and hearing the unusual commotion which was caused by a small portion of the palisade giving way, he had gone up the bank to see how things were going on, thus leaving the canoes unguarded, ready for Howe to take his choice. Howe swam across the little bay; reaching a small tree, he drew himself up by it, and lying flat on the ground pulled one of the light canoes towards him, and pushed it into the water without a sound. Then came the thought, if all the canoes were in the water their owners could not possibly pursue save by land. It required only strength and caution, both of which Howe possessed. Steadily he drew down first one and then another, till all but one canoe, and the two largest and lightest, which he had decided to take for Mrs. Dare, were floating away silently on the smooth water; then he carefully brought to the water his chosen two; the other lay among dry leaves on the bank, and he decided not to run the risk of its rustling betraying him. Fastening the two together, he stepped into one, and let the tide carry him far out before he used the paddle; no one had seen him, or heard a sound. The Indians always believed and declared that their canoes had been floated away by the water spirit, who was angry with them, but spared their medicine-man's canoe, which was the one that lay among the leaves. Howe was pretty well worn out when he reached the sheltered spot where the anxious watchers waited for him. He told them of his adventure, and that he felt very sure the palisade could hold out only a little while longer, and that he was too worn out to paddle them to Croatoan, but if they would wait only a few minutes more, he would go to the palisade and send some one to them.

"And you, Howe," Mrs. Dare asked, "what will become of you?"

The men will soon need a place to hide or retreat to, then I will bring them here. Thompson and Harvey will come back for us." He had hardly finished speaking before he was gone, and they sat quietly waiting.

Who would come, and when? The moments rolled on like hours. The night wind sighed in the pines till it seemed like a human moan. A great cry suddenly pierced the stillness; it was from the Indians, and yet it was not their war-whoop, rather a mournful cry. It sounded again and again, and then died away.

"Either they have discovered the canoes are gone, or they have broken down the palisade; you can rarely tell whether they are sorry or glad," Mrs. Dare said.

"If it is their canoes," said Mistress Wilkins, "they will come along the shore for them, and we shall surely be found."

"Let us still hope and pray," Mrs. Dare said feebly.

"Hark!" whispered Patience, "I am sure I hear some one coming." The twigs were cracking and the underbrush breaking. It was not Howe's decided step either. No, nor was it Howe's voice that said, "Mrs. Dare, your father left me in his place, to guide and govern his people. As none of them wish me to do either at present, I am sure he would say my duty was with you. Howe says we must go off at once."

She thanked him as he helped Mistress Wilkins and Patience into one canoe, and herself and the two babies into the other.

"The tide runs directly to Croatoan, so we can float most of the way without paddling," Gage said, as the canoes, fastened together, floated quietly away from the shore into the stillness and darkness of night.

Howe, after leaving the little party on the shore, went back to the palisade; he found the men fighting like true Englishmen, but he managed to explain to Gage the condition of the women; and then, after seeing him safely off, he went to work with a will: every one was needed.

The palisade was fast giving away, several large holes were plainly to be seen; the Indians were fighting with all the power of their wild, savage nature. If they once got through the palisade, every white man must die; then he thought of the women and children, and wondered if Manteo would receive them kindly, or if he would resent Ranteo's treatment. As he fought and tried to encourage the men, his thoughts ran on quickly. He thought of the future, and Governor White's return; who would tell him where to find what was left of the little colony? surely the three letters on the tree over the little bay would not. He slipped down from his place, having just thrown over his adversary whom he was fighting with hand to hand. Opening his pocket-knife, he found a large tree that would be easily seen, stripped the bark off about five feet from the ground, and on the smooth surface he carved in clear, old English characters, CROATOAN. He had just finished the " n," when a sudden pain made him lose his hold on the branch. He tried to raise himself to put the cross over the word, as the governor had said to do if in danger or distress, but he could not move. He could only lie there listening to the cries and war-whoops, and now and then a groan from a dying or wounded man. Above all, he could hear the sad call of the night heron ; he could see that the Indians had broken away the palisade and were rushing in. How many seconds before they would find him, he wondered. The vision of a gray stone church across the sea came before him, where he had learned from his very babyhood the truths and lessons which had made him a blessing and a credit to his country, and enabled him to lie there now facing death without a fear. He thought of the dear old face of his rector, remembered his last words at parting, and the promise of his prayers. " Such prayers must be heard on high," he muttered. "I have forgotten many of his holy teachings, but the dear Lord will be merciful and forgiving. He will, he will."

An Indian was coming very near; but what was that cry? It came from the Indians that were outside the palisade. Those who had forced their way in seemed to be retreating. He longed to ask, but there was no one near enough. Presently all became still, except for the low, sad wail that came from the outside. The white men were evidently astonished, but were taking advantage of the lull to patch up the palisade.

Presently a man came near, and asked, " Who are you?" Howe answered, asking at the same time, " What has stopped the fight? "

" That's more than we can tell," was the reply. " It's something on the shore, though ; something makes them think their gods are angry, for they have stopped fighting, and are offering gifts and dancing dances to one of their spirits. It is a good thing for us, anyway."

" Put any of the Indians that have been wounded or killed outside, then come back to

me," said Howe, "and I will tell you something."

After half an hour the man, came back, and
three others with him.

" Are you hurt ? " he asked.

" Yes," said Howe, " it's an arrow just above
my shoulder, I think, but it is broken off."

The men could feel the end of the arrow,
and with great difficulty, and causing him much
pain, they drew it out.

" How are our men ? " he asked, as soon as he
could speak.

" It's hard to tell exactly, but they're mostly
all wounded more or less, and there are thirteen
killed," was the answer.

" We must not stay here: we cannot tell what
those savages will do next; but first, we must
hide Governor White's boxes," said Howe.

There was a little silence, then one of the
men said, " We might as well tell you the worst,
you have got to come to it. We're all sorry,
but it can't be helped. There wasn't one among
'em like my old woman, 'Ilda, though the
'eathen dogs have done away with every woman
and child we 'ad."

Howe almost laughed as he replied, " I was
the heathen dog. I helped them to go to Croa-

toan, where we must go as soon as possible. That's what happened to the Indians in the middle of fighting; they must have suddenly discovered that their canoes were gone, and, I dare say, thought some of their gods had spirited them away."

" Thank 'eaven, thank 'eaven! " cried the first speaker, falling on his knees. " Thank 'eaven for my 'Ilda! "

They saw that Howe was exhausted, and left him resting on the ground while they went to work. An hour later Governor White's trunks were buried, and all the little treasures they could carry were packed in bundles, and all was made ready to leave Roanoke.

Howe and Barnes were both too seriously wounded to walk; they were laid on rude biers and carried. The dead men had been buried; others, who were only slightly wounded, walked, though in more or less pain. The way through the forest was a rough one, but their courage kept them up. At last the bank was reached, and in a sheltered hiding-place they found Thomson and Harvey waiting with the largest boat; the other, they said, had not reached Croatoan when they left. They had also sev-

eral of the floating canoes, which they had captured on their way back.   As day dawned, they
found all that remained of the English colony
on the shores of Croatoan, waiting to see how
the chief Manteo would treat them.

CHAPTER VII.

CHAPTER VII.

"She had eyes of sunniest English blue;
    She had tresses of golden hair;
  Her cheeks were tipped with the hawthorn's hue;
    Her name, Virginia Dare."

MANTEO, true to the faith he professed, forgave and forgot, or rather he never spoke of his warning, or Ranteo's strange visit to Roanoke; when he understood that the white tribe were in trouble, and had fled to him for protection, he solemnly held out his hand to Mrs. Dare, then handed her a long pipe, seeming to take it for granted that she filled her father's place. She went bravely at it for a few minutes in sight of all Manteo's warriors, who watched her with a strange awe; then he took the pipe from her and led her to a wigwam, where she was to stay while the refugees were provided for by the Indians.

The autumn days slipped by, and the winter came. It was a mild winter, even for that part of the country; and as it broke, and the first mild, balmy spring days came, the settlers began

83

to watch for the governor's return. Day after day they looked, but the mild spring melted into the heat of summer, and yet he did not come.

Hopeful Kent and his boat-load that left Roanoke in such a hurry that night had never been seen or even heard of; they had either been drowned, or captured by Wanchese's men. Autumn again began to paint the trees yellow and red, yet no sign of a sail; the men were growing discontented, and gave up watching for the ships they would never see, and went more ardently at their grumbling.

One night, nearly fifteen months after Governor White and his fleet had left the shore of Virginia, the men's discontent, which had been smouldering like a choked fire, burst into a blaze of defiant rebellion, and on that same night they slipped away in the darkness. Sixty of the men whom Manteo had sheltered and cared for more than a year went to Wanchese. Barnes was the leader in this, as in the former troubles ; but he did not tell the men all he meant to do ; he knew them too well to expect them to agree to anything so base as this plan. In truth, he meant to betray Manteo. Wanchese listened to his proposal with disdain and distrust, then he cried, " Such a dog shall not live ! " and with a blow of his tomahawk Barnes fell dead. Many of the men were killed, others were branded and kept as slaves.

Life was more quiet and peaceful after the discontented were gone. Of course there were sad hearts among the women and children for a while, for some had lost husbands and fathers. The weaker ones broke down utterly with the life of exposure and hardship. More than one grave had been made ; the Indians looking on in awe and wonder at the Christian burial. Mrs. Dare had learned many Indian words, and in a quiet way she had done much for the neglected women and children, for there were such among those poor savages, as there are to-day in our own civilized towns and villages; and in that way she won not only their hearts, but the hearts of the men also. There is no surer way in the world to a man's heart than through his children.

All this time the baby Virginia grew. The soft down on her round head had changed to a halo of golden curls. Her eyes had grown large and deep like the sea; sometimes a sparkling, laughing blue, and sometimes almost a gray when a cloud of sorrow crept

across her little horizon. She was not afraid
of anything, and nothing seemed to harm her.
The cold rain or the hot sun never made her
ill; she seemed to open like a flower, gaining
strength and beauty from all that nature gave.
One day when swinging in her willow cradle
under the blue sky, laughing and playing with
her toes, as children do, the old woman or
mother of the tribe, bent and wrinkled, browned
and weather-beaten, came slowly up the hill
with several of the squaws. Patience sat on
the ground holding the baby Elizabeth, who, as
soon as she saw the old squaw, gave a wild cry
of fear, and buried her face on Patience's
shoulder, moaning and sobbing. The old
woman shook her head, and passed on to the
willow cradle. Little Virginia looked up at
the ugly old face for some time, as if she were
studying it. Then she stretched out her tiny
white hands with a pretty baby laugh. The
squaw bent over the cradle; Virginia cooed and
smoothed the brown, wrinkled cheek; a murmur
of delight passed through the group of Indian
women. Mrs. Dare, who had come to the door
of the wigwam, lifted the baby from its cradle,
and tried to put her in the old Indian's arms;
but she drew back, clasping her hands and mut-

tering as she looked up towards the sky. The
other squaws acted in the same way. Ranteo, who had just come up, explained to Mrs.
Dare that his people had never seen a papoose
with blue eyes before, and they would not touch
it, for they thought it must be a spirit. From
that day Virginia received presents of all kinds,
from the skin of a bison to the wing of an eagle.
Her baby clothes were worn out long ago, and
she lay wrapped in skins, like any papoose.

She was a little more than a year and a half
old when Howe went with Gage to see if there
was any sign of Governor White's fleet. They
never came back. Life went on quietly at Croatoan. The men went to their hunt, or, in their
gaudy paint and war toggery, went to fight.
The women beat out their vessels, or wove bas-
kets, and dried skins. The children played
at their sham wars, or went on their imaginary
hunts, or sang their songs full of myths and
mysteries.

The summer that Virginia was three years old,
she was playing under the willow-trees outside
the wigwam with little Elizabeth, whom she
had nicknamed Beth, and whom she was truly
fond of; the only one in the world who loved
the fretful, delicate child with a love that was

not mingled with pity. They were playing quietly together, when a squaw, holding a little boy by the hand, came near and stood watching them. Beth at once stopped playing and began to cry, while Virginia smiled at the little boy, who was several years her senior, and held out her hand, saying, "Will you come play?" He came to her, but stood more like a soldier on duty than a child ready for play. The two looked curiously at each other for several moments. The boy, pointing to Virginia's great blue eyes and then to the blue bird he held in his hand, exclaimed, "Owaissa! Owaissa!" then he laid the bird on her golden curls; and when, after a long play, he went away, the squaw who had charge of him urged him to take the bird back, for it was the most loved of all his toys. He shook his head and angrily refused. He was Iosco, Manteo's son; and after that he came often to the willow-tree and played with Owaissa, as he called her. As she grew older and was able to play with Iosco and the other Indian children, she was known among them only as Owaissa.

Virginia was nearly six when Mrs. Dare began to give up all hopes of seeing the English ships that were to bring her husband and father.

The hard, rough life of exposure had made great changes in the young and beautiful woman who had sailed from England a happy bride only a little more than seven years before. She looked twenty years older; her wavy brown hair was gray; her complexion was burnt and sallow. She lived only for her little daughter, and what good she could do among the poor heathen, who fairly worshipped her. She had taught Virginia to read. When six years old, the child knew all the old familiar Bible stories, and she could sing many of the old hymns and and psalms. Thus the education of the first American-born child slowly progressed.

The squaw who waited on Iosco, whose name was Adwa, was very fond of both children: her own, she said, had all gone to the Happy Hunting Ground. She would tell them stories by the hour, while the three children sat listening breathlessly, for Virginia always insisted upon bringing Beth in for whatever was going on. As the squaw sat and parched the corn, she would tell them of Mondamin, and how the young Indian fasted and prayed for no selfish purpose, but for the profit of his people; and how he wrestled with and conquered Mondamin, because of his prayer to the Great Spirit. Or as they sat by the water she would tell them how the Puk-Wudjie fed the great fish, or how they killed Kwasind. Or they would watch the clouds clear away after a storm, and Adwa would tell them how the little flowers that died on earth bloomed again in the rainbow. As they sat in the growing darkness, watching the little fire-flies, she taught them the Indian children's good-night song : —

" Fire-fly, fire-fly, bright little thing,
 Light me to bed, and my song I will sing!
 Give me your light as you fly o'er my head,
 That I may merrily go to my bed.
 Give me your light, o'er the grass as you creep,
 That I may joyfully go to my sleep.
 Come, little fire-fly, come, little beast,
 Come, and I'll make you to-morrow a feast.
 Come, little candle, that flies as I sing,
 Bright little fairy-bug, night's little king.
 Come, and I'll dance as you guide me along,
 Come, and I'll pay you, my bug, with a song !"

Beth could not learn the song; in fact, she had learned very little of the Indian language, while Virginia spoke it quite as well as English. In return for Adwa's tales of Indian lore, Virginia would often tell the Bible stories she loved so well, old fables, or wonderful fairy tales; she even taught Iosco her favorite hymn. In this way the first six years of her life were passed, and her intellect and imagination were developed. In the same proportion she gained strength and vigor from the active games of the Indian children. She could climb a tree as nimbly as a squirrel, keep up with any child of her own size in the race, scramble down a steep cliff, or run over a narrow bridge formed only of a branch, as if she were in truth an Owaissa. Her life was light-hearted and sunny: no cloud of sorrow had yet obscured its baby brightness. But a dark cloud was fast gathering. Even when the cloud had broken away, the sun would never again be as bright as it had been before.

CHAPTER VIII.

CHAPTER VIII.

" O the long and dreary winter !
O the cold and cruel winter !
Ever thicker, thicker, thicker
Froze the ice on lake and river,
Ever deeper, deeper, deeper
Fell the snow o'er all the landscape."

LONGFELLOW.

THE winter after Virginia was seven years old was one which could never be forgotten by those who lived through it. The snow fell thick and fast for days together. Then came a cold wind, which blew until the streams were frozen like iron, and the great snow mounds became as mountains of shining metal. The wind sang dirges among the leafless trees ; the hunters went out day after day, and returned empty-handed ; the forest seemed deserted by all living things. The children cried for food, and not getting it, sickened and died. The women made fires and offered gifts to the Great Spirit of the Hunt. Manteo and his Christian people offered prayers daily. But all appeared to be of no avail.

95

Mrs. Dare was lying on her tussan of skins, and Virginia kneeling by her, with her arms tightly round her mother's neck. They were talking as they often did together. Virginia was saying, "But, mamma, why does God send trouble and sorrow and pain to us if he really loves us?"

"It is just because he does love us, darling, that he sends us sorrow to lead us to love him," was the gentle reply.

"But, mamma, dearest, you love God, yet he sends you so much pain. And you have not enough to eat, either. It cannot be to make you love him," said Virginia.

"Yes, my darling; we may love him all our lives, and yet not give him all the love we owe him. He never sends a pain or sorrow that is not for our good, though we cannot always know why it is. When you were a very little girl, almost a baby, and your gums were so sore, it was because I loved you and wanted to save you from pain that I lanced the sore place and gave you great pain just for a moment. You could not understand why then, even if I had explained it to you, but you never doubted my love. You knew I would not hurt you unnecessarily. We must trust God in the same way, dear, for he loves us even more than I love you."

"O mamma! you make me good; when I am with you I can do anything. I don't even mind being hungry;" and Virginia's great blue eyes were full of tears as she looked into her mother's face.

"Darling, you must learn to be good without me; we may not always be together, you know."

Mrs. Dare spoke with so much feeling that Virginia started and looked pained. But before she could speak, the skin that hung in front of the doorway was drawn aside, and Manteo came in. He sat down, with bowed head, and without speaking a word. Virginia, who had learned to love him, sat quietly at first. She knew he must be in very great trouble over the sufferings of his people, and her loving heart was full of sympathy.

At last she crept softly to him, and laid her curly head on his brown hand. Her eyes told more than words could express. With a great effort he raised his head.

"The Great Spirit, the mighty Werowance, has forgotten us, or he is angry. The people die, and there is no food. Manteo's own child

Iosco has the curse. There is no food to give him; he must die."

"No!" cried Virginia, "God will not let Iosco die. Have you asked him for food for Iosco, Werowance Manteo? I know he will save him."

"All night," replied Manteo, "under the stars on the cold snow did Manteo talk with God. But he would not hear him."

Mrs. Dare had risen. Manteo could not fail to notice how frail and ill she looked, as she came toward him. She drew the skin that lay over the couch around her as she said, "Manteo, take me to Iosco!"

He sprang up, a gleam of hope in his dark eyes. "Will the lady go to Iosco?" he cried. "Will she ask the Great Spirit to save the boy's life? Her god will hear her voice, though it be soft as a morning breeze in the budding time."

They passed out into the biting wind, the tall chief bowed with grief, the delicate English lady, and the sweet child with golden hair, and walked over the frozen snow to Manteo's wigwam. Mrs. Dare bent over Iosco as he lay on a tussan of balsam on the floor of the wigwam, restless with fever. She stroked the dark hair back from the flushed forehead, and then turning to Virginia, said in English, "Go and ask Mistress Wilkins to give you the red herbs, and bring them to me quickly, dear."

Virginia flew over the snow, and returned with the herbs in a small iron pot that had been brought from Roanoke, before the squaws crouching around the wigwam thought she had time even to reach Mistress Wilkins. Mrs. Dare stirred up the fire which was smouldering on the floor of the wigwam, prepared the herbs carefully, and boiled them in the iron pot. Poor Iosco lay gasping, delirious, and exhausted. Manteo thought he was dying, and caught Mrs. Dare's hand almost fiercely as he cried, "Ask the Great Spirit! Oh, ask him quickly!"

She knelt down quietly by the poor boy, Virginia knelt too, and all followed their example. There had been regular hours for prayer before Howe and Gage had been lost; since then, all were welcome who cared to come to Mrs. Dare's wigwam for devotions. She felt keenly a woman's dislike to put herself conspicuously before the world, even though it were a little heathen world; but she had taught them a great deal in a quiet way. They felt she was their friend; they knew and loved her. And now with her simple words of prayer every

heart in that rude cabin was lifted to the great
Father above.   Mrs. Dare gave Iosco the herb-
tea that had been simmering over the fire.   The
hot draught and her gentle ministration soothed
the poor boy, and he fell into a quiet sleep.
Manteo still knelt on the floor.   When he saw
his boy sleeping sweetly, he exclaimed, "The
Father is great and good, but he is angry with
the redman, and will not hear his voice.   Only
the voices of the Blue-eyes reach his camp."

"Oh, no!" said Mrs. Dare earnestly.   "Oh,
no, Werowance Manteo!   The great Father
loves us all, and he hears your prayers as soon
as you speak.   Ask him now to guide you, and
go to the forest and hunt, for Iosco must have
something to strengthen him when he awakes."

"Will the white lady speak to the Great
Spirit for Manteo while he goes and hunts?"
he asked.

"I will, indeed," she replied.   And Manteo
silently took his bow and arrows and left the
wigwam.

For hours Iosco slept peacefully.   At sunset
his father returned, to the great joy and delight
of every one, bringing with him the flesh of a
young bear.   Mrs. Dare prepared a dainty dish,
and told Virginia to give Iosco a little when he

first awakened, and to come and tell her how he was; that she was going back to her own wigwam for a while. Virginia was a very sensible little woman for only seven years old. She was born with the rare and blessed gift of a true nurse; and though there were five squaws in the wigwam, they let her sit close to the patient, feeling that she had a sort of supernatural power. They were afraid when her mother went away; but, as Iosco grew no worse, they decided Virginia must have the same power with the Great Spirit. When at last Iosco stirred and opened his eyes, one of them handed Virginia the food, that her hand might put it to his lips. He smiled at her as he took a little of the food, and then he went to sleep again. She slipped away to tell her mother the good news that Iosco was certainly better. Virginia stepped out of the wigwam into the cold night air. How the wind howled! The silver moonlight lay on everything, making the world in its white winding-sheet ghastly enough. The cold desolation seemed to freeze Virginia's heart. She shuddered as she ran on. Here was Beth coming to meet her. "Dear Beth, how good you are to come! Iosco is better. But what's the matter?" she asked, as Beth drew her toward the light that shone from the wigwam. Mistress Wilkins was there, and two old squaws, she saw as she reached the doorway. And her mother, where was she? A cry broke from Virginia as she saw her lying white and motionless on the bed. She threw herself on her knees, and laying her head on her mother's breast she cried again and again, "Mamma, dearest mamma! Oh, speak to me just once, your own little girl. Open your eyes, please! Do look at me, oh, please, mamma."

But the still, calm face lay against the black robe, in that peace which sorrow or pain alike are powerless to disturb.

A hemorrhage had come on just after she had left Iosco. She never spoke again, but lay with folded hands till the angel of death closed her eyes forever. Virginia was alone.

CHAPTER IX.

CHAPTER IX.

" To cure heartache is godfather Time's business, and even he is not invariably successful." — J. H. EWING.

WHEN great sorrow comes to us in youth, we feel it must affect and change the whole world; but when we have lived longer in this changeable world, we take it for granted that the whirl of life will go on as usual, only we ourselves drop out for a little while, to fight with our heartache alone, and to conquer it, with God's help, ere we take up the busy thread of our life again with placid faces, just as if our thread and shuttle were as bright and beautiful as before; and perhaps when all our work looks gray to us, we are weaving the most perfect and beautiful pattern.

Poor little Virginia had never thought of life without her mother, until that conversation which Manteo had interrupted; and then her mind was so full of Iosco's sickness that she did not think of her mother's words again until that

105

dreadful moment came when she called and called, and no answer came from those still lips, and she knew that her mother would never hold her in her arms again and kiss her. Everything went on just as before, except that the frost soon changed to a thaw, game became more plentiful, and the suffering less. But not so Virginia's sorrow: it was so deep and intense for a while, Mistress Wilkins thought it would wear her young life out. Beth was her great comfort through this lonely time: she was one to love, one who really needed her, and the two children truly loved each other. Iosco grew quite strong after a time: he never forgot what Mrs. Dare had done for him, and that it was in saving his life she had hastened her own death. He had always been fond of Virginia, and now his love was mingled with gratitude. There was hardly an hour of the day he did not bring some little offering for "Owaissa," or tell her stories, or sing songs to her. Time softens the greatest and sharpest sorrow. Let us thank God for it: we should die were it not so. Though Virginia's heart was nearly broken by her mother's death, and she wished that she too might die, she did not die, but took her life up bravely after a while; helping those among

whom she lived and whom she really loved;
gathering flowers and forest treasures in the
summer; watching the birds build their nests,
and the trees put on their pretty dresses in
budding-time; helping in the work, and playing merry games through roasting-ear time; in
the fall of the leaf gathering acorns and nuts,
and in winter sitting with others around the
wigwam fires of cedar-wood, and listening to
the stories which the old men told.

So the years passed by, and Owaissa grew
from a child to a girl. She was tall and
slender; her eyes had a more thoughtful expression than when she was a child, but in
other ways she was unchanged. She grew up a
perfectly natural girl, full of the poetry and
romance of the wild people of the forest. Iosco
was still her devoted friend: she looked upon
him as a brother. They wandered through the
forest together, gathering flowers or acorns or
sweet grasses. Sometimes they sat down and
rested on the banks of a little stream, and told
each other stories. Iosco's were of the wild
Indian lore. He told her of Odjibwa and the
Red Swan, of Hiawatha and his Minnehaha.
One day they sat on the bank of a little stream
which rushed on, making a tiny waterfall just

below, which sang to them; so Iosco thought, as he sat there with Owaissa, while overhead the pines waved their lofty branches, and the soft breezes whispered love-songs among them. Wild-flowers and delicate mosses nestled about their feet. All around, laurel blossoms made the forest beautiful and the air fragrant. Birds were flying to and fro, and from a near tree a whip-poor-will was singing to its mate, as if it were telling its love. Iosco was watching Virginia. She looked more like an angel than ever, as she sat with her golden hair falling in masses over her mantle of doe-skins, her slender hands clasped while she listened to the water and the birds.

Her eyes of deepest blue were looking thoughtfully far away. Iosco was fond of Virginia, very fond; but he never thought of her as he did of the Indian maidens. The moments he spent with her were the happiest in his life. When they walked hand in hand, a strange thrill passed through him. He would have died for her willingly, had there been any need. His quick eye saw now that she was sad as she sat listening; and he drew closer to her as he asked, "Where do Owaissa's thoughts go, that they send such sorrow out of her eyes?"

"Iosco," she said, "mamma would tell me if she were here, that I ought to be thankful for all God has given me. I often fancy when I sit alone that I can hear her telling me just as she used to, that it is one's duty not only to be contented, but to be cheerful and happy. I think I am usually, don't you, Iosco?"

He nodded as he replied, "Owaissa is like a bird, her eyes are so bright, her laugh is so merry."

"I try to be," she went on, "and I am very happy indeed. Every one is so kind to me; but sometimes I can't help wishing very much that I could see some of my own people. I should like to know if my father is alive, and if he sometimes thinks of me. He went away when I was only ten days old: I know he could not forget his baby."

They sat silently for a few minutes, then Virginia looked up into Iosco's face. "You know," she said softly, "sometimes I feel sure my father will come for me and take me away."

Had she felt Iosco's hand, she would have been astonished at its icy coldness, and would have wondered what made him clinch his fingers as if he were in pain. From that day a wild dread of the white man's return haunted Iosco.

An Indian never shows his emotion, so he only said quietly, "Did I ever tell Owaissa the story of Battao? It is a beautiful one from the far north, a captive of my father's told it to me."

"No: you never told it to me. I should like to hear it," Virginia said, with a little sigh.

Iosco would have made an ideal picture as he sat there. His black hair was thrown back from a high forehead, beneath which two dark eyes looked out, which were remarkable for their depth and truth. He had a straight, well-cut nose, and a mouth almost severe, so firm and decided was its expression. When he smiled, one forgot the stern look, for a sweet, gentle expression transformed the face. It was a classical face, and its owner had a deep sense and appreciation of the poetry of life. Certainly they made a study for an artist, — the fair girl with her golden hair, and the graceful figure of the Indian, as he told her the quaint old Indian legend.

"Many, many moons back, in the sunny north, over towards the setting sun, lived a mighty Werowance whom they called Tyee. His lands stretch all along the beautiful sound, where fine wampum is found. This Tyee had a daughter. The name of the beautiful maid was

Battao. Every one, even those far away, knew
of the rich wampum and the fine furs that would
belong to the man who should take Battao for
his wife. Her father said she should go to no
man whom she did not love, and he kept firmly
to this, though chiefs of great tribes came to
win her, and many from every part sought her.
Battao would look at none of them.

"One day a brave warrior came, tall and handsome. Battao looked at him, trusted his brave
eyes, and loved him. As they floated over the
smooth waters in Battao's swift canoe, they
came to a beautiful island, where they sat on
the shore and talked. And many days when
the sun had gone half-way on its journey, and
done its day's baking, so that the air was as
that which comes from the fire, Battao and her
maidens would cross to the beautiful island,
and there her lover would tell them strange
stories. As they listened, the maidens sifted
the soft sea-sand through their fingers, and as
it fell upon the shore it formed the shape of
whatever Battao's lover was saying; there it
hardened, and yet may be found, and it brings
the favor of all the gods to any one who finds
one of the forms and wears it in his wampum
belt."

" Oh, I should like to see some of the shapes, Iosco, wouldn't you?" asked Virginia.

" Yes," he said, "I should; and I should like to go to that land, it is so sunny, our captive said."

" It could not be more lovely than it is here," Virginia replied; "but please go on and tell me what became of Battao."

Iosco was happy for the present; at least he had made Owaissa forget the white tribe, and the canoes with pinions like wings, that she had said she was sure would come. So he went on gladly: —

"One day, when Battao, with her lover in her canoe, and all her maids in their canoes, were going back from the beautiful island, as they came to the deep part of the water, Battao's lover said some words to her in a strange language that the maiden could not understand, then sprang into the water. Battao did not cry out, she only looked down where her lover had disappeared; so did her maidens. But he did not rise, nor could they see anything of him, and they went home to their people. When they told the strange story, all the people said Battao's lover had drowned himself, and other men began to come every hour. But Battao

would not look at them or their presents, saying
that her lover was not dead, that he said before
he jumped into the water he would come
back in twelve days. None of her people believed Battao; and her maids went into the
wood, wailing and mourning for her loss. But
every day when the sun was half-way on its
journey, she would call her maids from the
wood and lead them down to the water. Then
they would paddle their canoes to the place
where Battao's lover had disappeared, and she
would look down into the water, in which she
could see the clouds, the sun, and even the trees
and mountains, all looking at themselves. She
saw not the brave and handsome lover until the
twelfth day came. And then, while she looked
down, he sprang up out of the shining water
into Battao's canoe."

"Oh, how happy she must have been!" cried
Virginia.

"Yes, very happy," continued Iosco, "and
all of Battao's people; for her lover brought
many presents with him, rare and wonderful
flowers that grow in the sea, and large pearls.
For Battao he brought beautiful coral. Then
there was a great happiness among all the people; for Battao and her lover were married. As

they paddled out in their canoe one day soon after, Battao asked her lover where he went to down in the water. He told her his people lived there, and he wanted her to go and see his tribe, where they hunted whales and seals, and gathered pearls and coral and beautiful shells, such as she had never seen. She took his hand, and together they sprang into the shining water. All the maidens, seeing the water swallow Battao up, gave a great cry that shook the whole forest. But she called out to them that she would come back to see her father. All her people mourned for her, and said some evil spirit must have taken her, and she must now be a fish in the water. But on the twelfth day she came to her people and to her father's wigwam, and told great and wonderful stories of the things she had seen. And she brought beautiful presents to her father, and to all her people. When she would go back, her father bowed down and grieved so that he would have died, but that she put her hand on his breast and promised him that while he lived his daughter would be with him six moons every year. And so she was; the rest of the time she was with her husband in the big seawater. But she still remembered and loved her people, and warns them of storms, even to this day, our captive said. She is seen over the place where she and her lover went down, and she looks tall and misty. No one dares come near her, for something dreadful has happened to all who have ever tried; before every dreadful storm she comes, and the people call the island to which she and her maidens went to listen to the lover's wonderful stories, the island of Battao."

They sat silently for a few moments, when Iosco had finished the story; then Virginia asked, " Do you think, Iosco, that all can tell whether they will love each other when they look at each other for the first time ? "

There was a strange look in Iosco's eyes, as he answered, "Iosco can tell little about such things, Owaissa ; some people surely could."

After another pause, Virginia said, " Your stories are so beautiful, Iosco, and I love them ; but they make me wish that I knew more of the stories of my people; there must be many that I have never heard, and even some of those my mother told me I have forgotten. I ought to have remembered them, and then I could tell you them, and teach you more about our God. I speak of him only to you, Iosco, for I know so little; I cannot even remember for myself; and when I try to talk to Mistress Wilkins about him, she shakes her head and says, 'Oh! he has forgotten us. If he loved us he would take us from this place ; don't speak to me about him, child, this is not his land. He cannot hear us when we speak to him. There is no priest or altar to hallow the land.' But, Iosco, when I am alone in the forest sometimes, and all is still, I can almost hear him speaking to me, and I feel and know that he is close to me, and I want so much to know him. I can only kneel down and say as mamma used, 'Dear Lord,' and I know he hears me. Beth or Patience or any of the others does not know as much as I: they have forgotten, or were never taught as I was, and you know I could not ask any of the men. Patience says they are the very worst that came over from England. I wish you knew, Iosco."

He did not reply; and they sat quietly together, only the song of the little birds above, and the sound of the falling water broke the perfect stillness.

CHAPTER X.

CHAPTER X.

"There are moments in life of real sorrow, when we judge things by a higher standard, and care vastly little what people say."—J. H. EWING.

"And the forests dark and lonely,
Moved through all their depths of darkness,
Sighed, 'Farewell.'" LONGFELLOW.

MANTEO was a wise and brave chief, as well as a good and thoughtful one, and was much loved by his people. The dozen Englishmen who yet remained as the remnant of the Roanoke settlers could not understand the reverence with which the savages treated their leader. His word was law. . His decisions were just, without regard to whom he was judging.

One autumn the twelve white men sat at their work of hollowing wooden bowls. As they worked, they talked about their future, and the prospect of seeing England again, which all confessed was very small.

"I tell you," said one, who looked strangely like Jack Barnes, and was, in fact, his brother, "I tell you what it is, fellows, we'll never see England if we wait for those lazy cowards to

119

come over for us. We must go over ourselves
if we are ever to get there."

The men all laughed; and one, Bill Smith,
said, " Why don't you tell us to swim over the
big pond? We're nothing but slaves here, anyway, and I'm sick of it. Having to obey a red
savage, an old heathen dog ! "

A third one, who really had the best face in
the crowd, replied, "I tell ye, lads, it's a bad
business, and that's true enough. But ye're not
bettering it by muttering about it. Manteo is
not a bad one, and ye forget he is not a heathen;
was he not christened by Master Bradford ? "

"That's all quite as you say; but it takes
more'n a few drops of water to make his ugly,
copper-colored skin clean, and a heap more to
make him a Christian, I'm thinking. I tell you,
Gray, you're easily taken in," Barnes said,
laughing. " I tell you what it is, lads," he continued, " if we're ever to go to England, we
must take the bull by the horns in the shape of
Manteo, and get rid of him. These red fellows
will not know what to do if he's gone, and we
can make 'em obey us. And we'll set 'em to
work at building a craft to carry us home."

As the men sat at work, their evil imagina-
tions and plans were making mischief faster

than their hands were making bowls. At the same time, not a great distance off, Virginia sat under the old willow-tree, working at the rude spinning that Mistress Wilkins had taught her. The day was beautiful, and she felt a strange sense of joy even in living. The world all about was so beautiful; as she spun, she sang, first one of the wild Indian songs, then an old English hymn that she remembered, though imperfectly. She sang and worked, as the sun played with her yellow hair and turned it into gold.

Her thoughts went far across the water. That great longing for her mother, then for her father, crept into her heart. Her hands rested idly. She must look out on the water. What if those great canoes should be coming in sight even now! There seemed to be an odd stillness, as if something were going to happen. She wandered along a little wood-path to a hill, beyond which she could see the clear water. There was the great blue sea, sparkling and dancing in the sunlight. Iosco had chanced to see the slight figure climbing the hill; he now stood watching her as the breeze played with her golden hair, and the clear blue sky formed a background. He knew what she was looking

for, and he was pained. Could she never be
happy with his people in their simple lives?
How could he expect it? But what was wrong?
The color suddenly died out of Owaissa's
cheeks; she clasped her hands as if in pain, and
sprang forward, out of his sight.

Hurrying up the hill, Iosco could see nothing
but Virginia's waving hair. She turned her
head, and even far away as he was, he could see
that her face was as white as the dove's down
in her mantle. Iosco caught only one glimpse
of it, then she was out of sight. He was an
Indian; one sight was enough. He knew
Owaissa was in trouble, and bending his body
slightly, he went swiftly across the little knoll.
Surely it must be the canoes with the pinions,
that he so much dreaded. There was the sea,
clear and blue, no sight of anything good or bad
on it; but a strange and awful sight was before
him, one which he never forgot.

There was Manteo's tall figure tied to a tree
like any mean captive. By him stood Barnes
and two or three of the roughest white men.
A little way off stood Gray and one or two
others, who seemed dissatisfied and distressed
at what was happening. In front, flushed with
anger and indignation, was Virginia. She was

speaking, he could hear her, more like an eagle defending her young, than a dove : "Shame on you, Barnes! Shame on you! Shame on you all, to touch the man who has saved our lives, and cared for us all these years! You are worse than the savages you despise. We have been safe, going in and out among them, and you dare to harm their chief. I'm ashamed to be one of you people!"

It would have taken a good deal to shame Barnes. He only muttered, "You are nothing better than a heathen savage yourself."

She turned fiercely towards him. Iosco could see her eyes flashing as she replied, "You make me ashamed of the white people who are left here. As you say, I am no better than these Indians, who are Christians indeed. They have given us food and shelter all these years, and what do we give them? No better? I wish I were half as brave, half as noble, as some of them are. You are not worthy to touch the old man whom you have bound. One cry would bring ten times your number of Manteo's men, who would kill you all, should they see their chief in danger." And she added, her eyes gleaming with excitement, "I will give the cry, if Manteo will not. And if one man is found here he will be killed, as he deserves."

Barnes drew a knife from his belt as he came towards her, saying, "If you dare open your mouth, I will soon silence you. Try me!"

A slight rustle, a swift movement, and Iosco stood before Barnes, who shrank before the tall figure, and every white man fled. Virginia sprang to Manteo. With Iosco's knife she cut the cords that bound him to the tree. She kissed his hand where the cord had torn the flesh. The old chief was moved by her gentle, caressing care, and showed more feeling than when he was threatened with death. She knelt there by the old man, trying to show her love. Iosco stood at a distance, with folded arms, looking far away. He was thinking, surely this would make Owaissa forget the canoes with wings, when a sudden cry made him turn. It was Virginia; she sprang up as if to shield Manteo, who tottered a moment, then fell heavily to the ground.

"An arrow, Iosco, an arrow!" she cried, as she knelt by the prostrate form. Iosco bent down, his expression unchanged, save for a strange look in his dark eyes. He heard his father heave a deep sigh, then all was still.

Manteo was dead. The arrow had pierced his heart; but where had it come from? Iosco sprang up, the savage thirst for vengeance throbbing through his veins. With his hand on his tomahawk, one moment he stood looking down on his dead father, by whom Virginia knelt, her face rigid with horror. Looking up, she saw Iosco so changed she hardly knew him. He was staring at her, though he did not see her. She thought his anger and vengeance were turned on her. The scene of horror had changed her from a merry girl to a woman. The voice in which she spoke was deep and clear.

"Iosco," she said, "kill me if you will. I would die a hundred times over if I could bring back the life of the great and good Werowance who saved us. God will reward him. I know he will; and he will punish us. Nothing you can do to me will be hard or cruel. I will die any death you choose."

Iosco turned quickly away. He had forgotten Virginia until she spoke; he was absorbed in the dreadful thought of his father's death, and the idea that he had been killed by men whom he had not only saved, but had treated with every kindness. His only comfort lay in the thought of vengeance. But Virginia's words brought back his better self. He could not look at her, and turned away to hide his grief. There came before him the memory of Mrs. Dare sitting under the willow-tree, while he, Virginia, and the other children listened to her telling a story. He thought he could hear her saying, "Those very men whom he came to save, whom he loved and lived for, nailed him to the tree, pierced his dear hands and feet, and while they were doing it, they mocked and spit at him, and called him vile names. He was greater than any chief you ever saw or heard of. But he did not get angry. He was only so sad. Even in the moment of greatest pain, he looked up to his Father, the Great Spirit, and said, 'Forgive them, for they know not what they do.'"

Iosco felt he could have forgiven anything done to himself. But was it right to think of forgiving his father's murderers?

The answer seemed to come in Mrs. Dare's words again: "The dear Jesus could have killed every one of those men, and come down from off the cross; but he would not, for he loved us so much he was willing to bear all, to teach us how we could forgive each other. He not only forgave them, but asked his Father to forgive them also."

The breeze, the morning sunlight, the little birds, and the dancing waves, all seemed to be saying over and over to him, "The dear Jesus could have killed every one of those men; but he loved us all so much he was willing to bear all that to teach us how we could forgive each other." Was it, then, such a great thing to be able to forgive? He knew he could have every one of those pale-faces killed; every one would expect it. He never for one moment included Virginia when he thought of the white people. To him she was a being all by herself. As he turned, he saw her kneeling by the dead body, her hands clasped, her face upturned. It was white as marble. She must be speaking to the Great Spirit. Those treacherous hands could strike her from where they had struck his father. For the first time Iosco saw they were in danger, and he sent forth a great cry into the forest, which he knew would bring his people. Virginia knew what it meant. She rose and stood waiting.

CHAPTER XI.

CHAPTER XI

CHAPTER XI.

"Tis sweet to stammer one letter
Of the Eternal language — on earth it is called Forgiveness."

LONGFELLOW.

OH, that dreadful day! The howls and cries of the men, women, and children, as they came in reply to Iosco's call, and saw their chief, their father, lying dead! They also saw Virginia, motionless, as if she had been carved out of stone, standing over the dead. He had been their faithful Werowance. They stood aghast, unable even to fancy who could have done the dreadful deed. The medicine-man said solemnly: —

" The great Werowance rested under the arbor of wild vines that shade the wigwam, and as he lay on the mat in the heat of the mid-day sun, a pale-face stood before the Werowance, saying he had somewhat to speak, but must speak it with naught but pale-faces to hear, for it was a secret or charm of their tribe. Werowance was true, and trusted him: he went into

131

the heat and sun, following the pale-face. No man has seen him till now, when he clings to the earth. Why came not the pale-faces at the call of the Werowance?"

A mighty shout rose from the people as they moved around the body, and around Iosco, who stood with folded arms and faced the scene. Then the tumult ceased. The oldest of the company came forward; taking Iosco's hand, he put it first to his head and then to his heart, and so gave his oath of allegiance to the new chief. The others did likewise, till all the men had pledged themselves. Then they stood in silence to hear what he would say.

Iosco was a true Indian: he would have scorned to show deep feeling in his face or manner. He said, very quietly and calmly, " Carry my father to the wigwam."

They moved quickly to obey him. An old Indian put Manteo's pipe in his hand that it might be ready for him on his way to the Happy Hunting Ground. A young brave who had hated Virginia always, because as a child she had shown a preference for Iosco, now seized her arm to drag her away. But a strong voice made him stop.

"Stay, take thy hands off!" Then leaning

forward, Iosco said, "No Indian man shall touch a whiteskin save a man of full size."

Virginia noted his strangely altered face. Oh, he must be very, very angry, she thought! Surely he would never speak to her again. But he was coming towards her. He took her hand and led her away.

The sun dipped low in the west, sending a crimson glow through the forest; the birds chirped their good-nights to each other as they swung on the branches of the great trees. Perfect peace seemed to rest on everything. Iosco stood on the bank of the lake; on its smooth surface the glory of the sky was clearly reflected. A slight noise made him turn. Virginia stood by him, her face upturned, her beautiful eyes fixed on him wistfully.

"O Iosco!" she cried, coming nearer, "forgive me for disturbing you; but, dear Iosco, I am so sorry, so very sorry for you, and so ashamed of my people. I must tell you only this once, that our people at home would thank you if they could only know what you have done. We deserve to be killed. If the big canoes ever come over, full of white men like my father and grandfather, who, I am sure, must have been as good and brave as Manteo, — whom they loved, you know, — if they ever come, Iosco, tell them what he did for us, and please ask them for my father, and show him where my grave is, and my mother's also."

Her voice faltered, but she still stood looking steadily at him; there was nothing weak or sentimental about her; she was a brave girl, and meant what she said, every word of it. She knew the wickedness of the deed which her people had been guilty of, not only murdering without cause, but murdering the one who had sheltered and defended them. She took it for granted that Iosco was very angry. She thought it must make him feel enraged even to look at her. But when he turned and looked into her eyes, she saw no vengeance in his face. He took her hand and pressed it to his lips and to his heart. The color rose to her white cheeks, and her eyes filled with tears, which rolled down over her flushed face, and fell upon Iosco's hand. She let him draw her closer, and as she looked up she could not understand the expression in his dark eyes: it frightened her, yet there was nothing angry or fierce, there was a new, strange tenderness.

He said simply, " Owaissa, Owaissa! " as they stood there together. The sun sank out of sight and the rosy glow was gone. The still water of the lake showed only the reflection of the moon, and the two figures, one tall and dark, with rich mantle and wampum belt, the other, fair and slender, with a robe of woven turkey feathers lined with down from the breast of the wood-dove. They stood close together under the clear heavens, as they had often done ever since they could remember; but it was so different. What made the strange difference, neither quite knew. At last Virginia stole softly away.

The birds had gone to bed, and the moon was high in the sky, sending down a soft silver light over the great forest land. It looked at the little lake with its smooth water on which the two figures had been reflected at sunset. Now it showed only one. He stood alone with folded · arms and bowed head. For a long time he had stood there, even while the shadows cast by the moon were lengthening. Then he walked quickly up and down the bank. The tiny waves lapped his moccasins, but he heeded them not. At last, as if worn out with his solitary struggle, he threw himself on the ground, and lay so still, he looked more like a dead than a living form. There alone, with only the screech of the owl in the forest, or the call of the heron to break the stillness, in the dim light of the moon, alone with nature, Iosco was struggling with himself. He seemed to be two beings; one, the better self which Mrs. Dare's teachings had awakened, which saw and dimly realized the light and glory of the living Saviour; the other being, an Indian, with all the passion and vengeance naturally found in the descendant of a long line of fierce and warlike chiefs, whose creed was, two eyes for one eye, and always revenge, though it be waited for a long time, even from generation to generation. This being seemed to urge relentlessly: "They have slain your father; make them pay for every drop of his blood with a scalp!" The better self said over and over again, "He loved us all so much, he was willing to bear all this to teach us how to forgive each other. The dear Lord could have killed every one of those bad men." The first voice, almost in reply, seemed to say, "If you get rid of all the other pale-faces, you can keep Owaissa always. You can easily conceal one, while a number would be discovered if the great canoes should come looking for them. If you do not have these men killed, your braves will do it. It is not safe for them here. Even as a tiger steals her prey they will be seized." And yet, in the darkness two great blue eyes seemed to look wistfully at him. He could hear the dear girl's voice, sweet and soft as the voice of a bird, saying, "God must be very angry with us. I know he will punish us, and he will reward Manteo." Was God really going to punish and judge? he wondered. The voice of the better self seemed to be saying, "If you could not keep them here, you could perhaps send them away somewhere else." Ah, yes! there was the great Werowance Powhatan, in whose friendship and esteem his father had stood very high. He might be glad to have some more workers in his tribe. These white people had introduced many things among his people, Iosco knew; a wonderful manner of spinning, and various other things. The captives, for such they now were, must be out of the way before morning, and no one must know where they had gone. How could he get them off unseen?

He rose. The struggle was over: the better self had conquered; but the fight had been a hard one. As he walked through the forest he mused. Should he tell Owaissa, or let her discover that they were gone in the morning? He never thought of including her in the party that were to go; and yet, why not? If it were unsafe for the other whites, might it not be unsafe for her? Would she not want to go with her people? She belonged to them.

He passed through the little village; all were sleeping; even the night itself seemed awed by the dreadful deed of the day. There lay the great Werowance Manteo. On the ground by the bier Virginia had thrown herself.

As he looked at her, she stirred, sighed, and muttered something. He caught his own name, the rest was indistinct.

"The Owaissa is like unto the angels she used to say were guarding our Werowance!" It was Ranteo's voice. He was on watch, fortunately for Iosco's plan.

"Ranteo knew my father when he was made a Christian; Mrs. Dare has told me about it. When the white man put the water on the Werowance's head, Ranteo was by his side. It was in the moon before the great canoes went over the water with all the white hearts, who left the pale-faces with black hearts behind," Iosco said.

"To kill us," the old Indian muttered.

Iosco continued, "Christians forgive those who do them harm, so I am going to do what a Christian would; I am going to let all the pale-faces go away, and not harm them. The son of

Manteo the Christian will be Christian too. Will Ranteo help him?"

Ranteo looked more surprised than if the skies had fallen. Then he walked over, and stood looking at Virginia for some time; coming back he said, "In that dark night long ago, when the child crouched on the rock to save Ranteo, as a dove might try to save an eagle, the pale lady spoke, and Ranteo promised to be the friend to her child," he said, pointing to Virginia, "and he will keep that promise now."

"Thinks Ranteo that Owaissa must go too?" Iosco asked. The old man shook his head. "It is not safe for a dove to be with hungry foxes. The white dove must go," he said.

An hour later a little group stood on the bank of the James River, known then as the Powhatan flu, on which they were to fly to safety. Iosco was to go with them till daybreak, when he was to return, and send Ranteo to guide them the rest of the way to Powhatan, on the Yough-hianund flu. They were to conceal themselves during the day. The moon was far on its way, but it smiled on them as they glided swiftly over the smooth water.

CHAPTER XII.

CHAPTER XII.

"I hold him great who for love's sake
    Can give with earnest, generous will;
But he who takes for love's sweet sake,
    I think I hold more generous still."

Proctor.

NEWS came from Ranteo, just as Iosco was starting on his return to Croatoan, that the whole tribe had risen up against him for helping his father's murderers to escape, and they would not have him for their chief. This was the doing of the medicine-men, who had lost much of their former power since Manteo's visit to England, for he had given up many of the old superstitions. Ranteo strongly urged Iosco to go on to Powhatan, and if he were received kindly, to stay there for a while; if his people needed him, Ranteo would let him know. He felt certain they would soon want him, for Meninosia, Manteo's brother, who was now to be chief, was hard and cruel. So it came about that Iosco reached the camp of the great Powhatan on the Youghianund flu at Werowocomoca, in company with the miserable remnant of the

English Roanoke Colony. It was at dusk when
he made known who he was, and they were ad-
mitted into the camp, and told that the great
Werowance would see the son of the brave warrior, Manteo, when the sun next stood over the
tall pine-tree. The next day was rainy, so the
medicine-men said the sun was not there, as they
could not see it, and Iosco was obliged to wait
till the following day, when the sun came out
bright and clear, and the whole world seemed
shining with unusual lustre. The fugitives
would know their fate soon. At noon Iosco
would be summoned to the great Werowance.

The sun had just come above the horizon as
Virginia stepped out of the wigwam, the birds
were singing their morning hymn, the little
squirrels were scampering to and fro getting
food for their young; a few of the women were
beginning to work at skins, others were prepar-
ing food. They looked curiously at Virginia as
she passed them, but did not speak, for she
looked sad, and they were sorry for her. She
must be the wife of the young chief, they thought.
But where did he find a squaw with eyes like
the sky, and hair like the sun? She passed under the shadow of the great pines alone. All
the world seemed to be in families, or at least to

belong to some one, while she was all alone. She had never known a relation but her mother. Oh, for that mother! why could she not have gone with her?

Virginia had lived long enough among the Indians to learn to restrain any display of feeling. And yet the thought of her mother in that sad, lonely hour was too much. She did not cry out, or even sob, as another English girl would have done. She only sank down at the foot of the great pine, covering her face. A little moan of "mother," seemed to shake her whole frame. Then she lay there so motionless that the little birds flew about her and never noticed her. Hundreds of miles across the water her thoughts travelled to her father. What could he be like, and where must he be? Would he ever come for his poor child? Oh, how she longed for him, that father whom she had never seen! Must she die alone here? And if she should die, would she go to her mother? She hardly knew the great God to whom her mother had gone. Would he know her? Or was it really as Mistress Wilkins had said, that he would not listen to the prayers of his children in a heathen land? Did it not really belong to him? Then she fancied she was sitting on her mother's lap, and listening to the wonderful story of the creation, and her mother saying, "After sin had come, God's sorrow was so great that he promised to send a Redeemer, which would be his own dear Son, and he would come to save us all." If he was, then, such a loving Father, he could not forget one of his children, and if he made the whole world, it must all belong to him. All these people must belong to him too, and they did not even know him. Perhaps she had been sent to teach them. Why hadn't her mother been spared a little longer to teach her? Oh, for some one to tell her over again what she had heard from her mother when she was too young to remember or understand it!

An earnest prayer for guidance rose to her lips. There were no special words, only the cry of the child to the Father whom she felt was listening. She had clasped her hands, and was looking up so earnestly that she did not see the bushes drawn aside and a young Indian maid, a mere child of nine or ten, step out and then draw back and look at her curiously. Hearing a sound among the leaves, Virginia turned, and saw the child also looking up to see what was there to gaze at so earnestly.

She was a strangely beautiful little figure as

she stood there, one foot raised as if to step forward, but resting still on the root of a great tree that rose some distance out of the ground. She wore a robe or mantle of fur, for it was only May, and the Indians are never in a hurry to change their few articles of clothing; besides, it had been the gift of her brother, whom she had loved dearly. The mantle was loosely girded, and fell low on her shoulders, over which masses of dark hair fell in dusky profusion. Her dark eyes were full of wonder at seeing Virginia, and at her strange position. Both looked at each other for a moment, wondering who the other could be. Then the Indian child sprang forward like a young deer, and threw herself on the ground by Virginia, and looked tenderly in her face, her great eyes full of pity, as she held out a garland of red flowers which she had been holding.

Virginia took it with a smile; but the child snatched it back, and bound it about Virginia's head. Then she drew back, pointed to the wavy golden hair and blue eyes with a strange look of awe, and clasped her hands, and bowed very low. Virginia caught one of the brown hands. She said laughingly, "I am not a goddess or a spirit, I am only a girl. Who are you?"

The child did not now draw her hand away. She said in a pretty way, putting her head on one side, "It is Cleopatra, the daughter of Werowance Powhatan, the sister of Nantiquas, the bravest, strongest Indian who ever shot an arrow." As she spoke, a bird-call sounded through the forest. She answered it almost exactly. There was a crackling and breaking among the bushes, and a young warrior stood before them.

"Does not the fairest little maid go to the Great Father, when all are gathered to see the mighty wonder which is like a linnet with a finch's bill, the captive from Croatoan, with eyes from the sky and"— But seeing Virginia, he stopped.

The sunlight peeping through the trees fell on Virginia's hair till it shone like gold. They stood looking at each other for several moments. Then the Indian maid took Virginia's hand and pressed it to her breast. Nantiquas at once did likewise, and then said, "The one with eyes from the sky belongs to the Spirit. Means it evil or good to the camp of the mighty Powhatan? He is a brave Werowance." And he took his sister's hand as she stood beside him.

"I do not belong to any spirit," Virginia said,

smiling; "I came with the white people whom Iosco, the son of Manteo, is seeking shelter for, and my forest name is Owaissa."

"Owaissa looks more like her namesake than like the white tribe whom the great Werowance is now to hear of," replied Nantiquas.

"Is the sun at the top of the tall pine? Oh, I must go to Iosco; where is he, can you tell me?" Virginia asked, almost passing them in her eagerness.

"Nantiquas will take the Owaissa maid to the wigwam of the Werowance Powhatan; the brave Iosco sits before the door." As he spoke, he turned and led the way, and the maidens followed him. Virginia could not help noticing how tall and handsome he was, his long black hair pushed back from his high forehead. He wore a skin girded about his waist with a belt of wampum. Over his shoulder hung a quiver of arrows, and on his left arm he carried a bow. In his belt he wore a tomahawk, and across his forehead was bound the skin of a green serpent, its bright eyes gleaming over his left temple. From his right ear to his waist was fastened a long string of pearls.

A strange sight was the wigwam or bower in which Powhatan held his court. He sat on a couch, which looked not unlike one of our modern bedsteads. It was made of fine wood, rudely carved with strange devices. He wore a robe of raccoon-skin, with a belt of the rarest wampum. His powerful arms were decorated with metal bracelets. The ground around him was strewn with dried sweet grasses and crushed pine-needles that made the air fragrant. At his head and feet sat two beautiful maidens. A hundred bowmen formed, as it were, the wall or outside of the court-chamber. In front of them were a hundred women with bare necks and arms, which were dyed with paccoon and decorated with white coral. Beside the great Werowance sat a beautiful girl about twelve or fourteen. (She looked like Cleopatra, and was, in fact, her sister Pocahontas, known to her people as Mataoka.) She gazed wonderingly at Virginia as Nantiquas and Cleopatra led her in, and she took her place among the wives and daughters that sat at the head of Powhatan's couch, on the right side of which, on mats, were seated the priests, or medicine-men, singing a queer dirge, keeping time to the melody with their grotesquely painted bodies. The curious song continued while Iosco entered. He was in the dress of a prince, wearing a white skin girded with his father's rare and beautiful wampum belt, in which was supposed to rest a great charm. On his feet he wore moccasins made of skins and beautifully wrought with queer patterns. Across his forehead were bound some rare and beautiful feathers, which rose high above his tall figure and nodded gracefully as he moved. He was attended only by one of his braves and three of the whites, who were dressed as Indians, and carried the presents he had brought from Croatoan, which they had now laid before him. An odd medley enough they were — a coil of deer sinews, a small belt of wampum, a string of noughmass, and last, but not least in the eyes of the chief, an old rusty English sword.

The chief did not deign to notice the things till the sword was put down, then he extended his great hand, and picked it up with a gleam of delight in his small, dark eyes as he held it. He took from his mouth his long pipe, passed it to Iosco, who smoked for some moments in silence. Then Powhatan nodded to Iosco, who returned the pipe and began his tale, not as if he were making a petition, but as if he were chanting or reciting a story. He told first of Manteo's going to England, then of the white men com-

ing to Croatoan; of the years that had passed
since, when they had lived in peace together;
then of his father's death, and the anger of his
people, and his wish to remain or leave the two
dozen pale-faces that were yet alive at Werowocomoca. He spoke of their skill in many
things not known to the Indian people.

He told it in a sing-song drawl, as if he did
not care in the least. But when the medicine-
men began to mutter, " They are ghosts; have
none of them; they kill," Powhatan looked at
the three white attendants, who certainly were
weird looking, with their yellow, grisly faces,
their colorless eyes, and white skins, and shook
his head unfavorably.

Iosco looked anxiously over at Virginia. It
was evident she was his chief anxiety; but
she, mistaking his look, thought he wanted her,
and sprang to him, saying, "Must we go, and
where?"

Powhatan half raised himself to look at her,
as she clung to the tall figure, fixing upon him
her great blue eyes, her wavy golden hair falling
loosely about her. Even the medicine-men
stopped their muttering, and the beautiful prin-
cess Mataoka bent over her father and whispered
something in his ear. He could not but admire

her beauty, old savage as he was, and he nodded to his daughter, who led Virginia away to her own wigwam. Then he ordered food to be brought to Iosco, which was his way of showing his welcome. And Iosco knew that he and his party were safe for the present.

CHAPTER XIII.

CHAPTER XIII.

"She was lost in a country new and strange,
   With lakes and with mountains high,
With forests wide, where the redmen range,
   And shores where the sea-birds fly."

FAIR and lovely was that sunny Virginia country. No wonder the ships went back to England with fairy tales. No wonder that, in spite of mishaps and disasters, there were always more of the quiet English folk ready to sail for the new world of romance and beauty.

The early spring melted into summer; the trees were festooned with wild vines; the forest was alive with flowers and birds. It was an ideal day in June, and the whole world seemed glad and happy. Virginia and the lovely princesses, Mataoka and Cleopatra, had gathered their arms full of flowers and berries. Virginia was twining them into garlands, as they sat by a little stream down which a canoe was gliding swiftly. It stopped near them, and Nantiquas, who was paddling, drew it upon the bank and sat down near Virginia, listening to her merry chatter with his sisters, till they sprang up to run after a butterfly.

He had been silent. Then he spoke eagerly, "Owaissa cannot tell what Nantiquas saw when he watched the big sea-water from the great salt oak."

"What did you see, Nantiquas? Please tell me," Virginia asked, dropping her flowers with a strangely anxious expression, which made Nantiquas feel that she knew, or imagined, what he had to tell her.

He replied quite indifferently, "As the waves from Witch's reef came to Nantiquas, there came with the waves a great canoe with wings. So close to Nantiquas it came, that the pale-faces shone as they put their irons in the sea. Even as they went down from the big canoe and dropped into a little one, the waves brought another big canoe, as one bird finding a carcass attracts many birds."

As he finished speaking, the color rose to Virginia's cheeks, then died away, leaving them deadly pale. Her hands were clasped. One moment she raised her eyes, her lips moved. Then she turned to the young Indian with a look that he never forgot, and said, "Nantiquas, in one of those must be my father; may I go and see them?"

"Owaissa could never walk so far. Nantiquas would take her, but the canoe is too small."

Nantiquas felt sure if her father were among the pale-faces he had seen, he would surely come and take her away, and this thought was not pleasant to him. So he did not mean to help her. But a feeling of jealousy rose in his heart when Virginia said, "Iosco will help me, I must go and find him, and tell him; I know he will be glad."

As she sprang up to go away, Nantiquas caught her hand. "Will Owaissa let Nantiquas go for her to the camp of the pale tribe and find her father?"

"Oh, how good you are!" she cried, her cheeks glowing, and her eyes sparkling. "But the white men will never know what you want. You cannot talk their language, and they may think you mean them harm." Such a sad, disappointed look came into her face that Nantiquas, seeing it, would have risked death a hundred times for her.

He drew himself up proudly, as he answered, "The son of Powhatan is not a fawn. He will go. Owaissa will tell him the words, and he shall say them to the white chief in the chief's own tongue."

" Do you think you could ? " she said, looking up wistfully into his face. " Could you say ' White ' ? "

He repeated it after her, " White."

" That is it ! " she cried, catching his hand in her delight. " That was my grandfather's name. He was a great man, a chief I think. Now, my father's name was Dare, and something else that was long and hard to say. But Dare will do; can you say it ? "

" Dare," repeated Nantiquas, still holding the little hand that had been put in his.

" Now, Nantiquas," she continued, "my real name, the one they would know me by, is not Owaissa. Iosco gave me that name when I was a little girl, because my eyes made him think of the Owaissa. It is my forest name, mamma used to say. But my name with my own people is Virginia; after the land I was born in, mamma used to say; but I don't understand how that can be, for I was born on the island of Roanoke. I was too young to think about it, or ask mamma how it was, before she went away. It is a hard word — Virginia, but do you think you can say it, Nantiquas ? "

Indians have a superstition that any one knowing the secret of the private name of a maid can work charms and witchery about her. So to Nantiquas it was a solemn, if not a sacred thing to repeat the word Virginia. But he did it quite correctly, and she clasped her hands with joy. "Say it all over once more, please," she urged. And he repeated clearly, "White, Dare, Virginia; does Nantiquas say it as Owaissa does?"

"Oh, yes," she said enthusiastically. "When will you go, Nantiquas?"

"Nantiquas will go even as the canoe waits by the water. Does Owaissa wish it?"

"Oh, will you? And come back quickly with my father, won't you? I won't tell Iosco anything about it, and we'll surprise him when you come."

Nantiquas pushed the canoe out from among the willows, and stepped in. As Virginia stood watching him, more like a beautiful spirit than ever, he thought, he saw her take up a sharp shell that she had used to cut the flowers that were too stout to break, and drawing her curls over her face, she cut one off with the shell and handed it to him, saying, "If you should forget the words, Nantiquas, or my father could not understand, or they would not believe you, you can show them this. They will know it did not come from an Indian maid, and they will be willing to come back with you, I know."

He took the silky yellow curl almost reverently. Catching her hand that had held the curl, he pressed it to his heart, then paddled down the stream into the Youghianund flu, and was soon out of sight. Nantiquas was not the only one who had seen the ships.

As Virginia went through the forest singing, her heart was very light and happy. She soon met Cleopatra and Mataoka, who put their arms about her. Cleopatra said softly, "Does Owaissa know that a great canoe is in the flu full of white men, and another one on the water of the Che-sa-peack?"

"Yes, dear Cleopatra, I know it, and it must be my father has come for me at last. I can hardly wait for him to come. But he will be here soon, I know."

"Owaissa will not go and leave us, oh, no, no! Owaissa will never leave us," and Cleopatra threw her arms about Virginia, and laid her head on her breast, her beautiful eyes full of love.

Virginia kissed her brown cheek as she answered, "If the great Werowance Powhatan should come for his pretty little Cleopatra, would she not go with him? She would go, but she would not forget her friends that she had left behind, or cease to love them just the same, and send them presents to show her love. What will my dear little Cleopatra have from sunny England?"

But the little Indian girl only clung closer, saying, "Cleopatra wants only Owaissa, and no present. Her love is in Owaissa's bosom, not in toys."

The whole camp was in a state of excitement over the strange news of the ships in the river. It was twenty years since Governor White had left Roanoke, and no Englishman had come since their sad fate. When the Governor returned to look for his colony, his ships had been in sight a few days from Powhatan's shores. But these present intruders, as many of the Indians called the pale-faces, evidently intended staying, for upon landing they began preparations at once for a camp, so the report ran.

Virginia listened in breathless silence to an old Indian who was telling all he had seen of the arrival of the English fleet; for it was, in fact, the colony which had embarked in their ships on the 19th of December, 1606, from Blackwall, near London, and had been for more than five months on their voyage, commanded by Captain Newport.

The old Indian sat smoking on his mat, resting after his long hunt, and hasty return to tell the news, which he was now doing for the third or fourth time, to the crowd of excited listeners. The men sat or stood, smoking, the women worked the skins on the ground, while one or two ground mondawmin, or Indian corn, in basins made of hollowed stones. These worked at a little distance, lest their noise might disturb their lords and masters, and were content with what fragments they could gather of the story that was being told.

" The eyes of Ramapo see far on the great sea-water, white wings as of a mighty sea bird. The wings come near, and he sees the pale-faces' canoe. Ramapo goes into the great tree; he sees the white man come to the land. He sees the canoes without wings pulled up. He sees, after the sun passes a bit, the pale-faces all stand under the trees, and one, the medicine-man, talks out of a book. They all kneel, then stand, some do look at the clouds, and some do hide their faces, that even the sun may not see them. Ramapo says, they talk to the Spirit that is in the clouds; and then he comes away"

"They were talking to God, Ramapo," cried Virginia, her great eyes full of tears, "the Spirit that lives in heaven, but loves and watches over us. It is he that has brought them to find me; I know it is. My father must be one of them. Did you see a man that looked like me, Ramapo?"

"Ramapo was too far to see the eyes, but surely he saw none with such hair, though many of the pale-faces seem ashamed of their skin, and wear much hair on their chin and cheeks to cover up the whiteness," was the old Indian's reply.

In their excitement they had not noticed the gathering clouds till the rumbling thunder made them see the storm which was just breaking over them. The awful stillness that often comes before a tempest seemed suddenly to enfold the forest. Not even a leaf rustled. The stillness could be felt but not described, and this little group of wild people, always in sympathy with the moods of the forest, stood as if listening, when suddenly the chanting or crying of the medicine-men was heard, and in the stillness the strange weird noise sounded clearly and distinctly. "The pale man, the murder man, he will kill, but the mighty Powhatan will lay him low. Away with the white faces out of the land, out of Powhatan's hunting-grounds, out of his sight, out of his sight! As the rabbit and the deer shall we hunt them, their hair shall we scalp."

Six of Powhatan's best bowmen came quickly forward, and without a word seized one of the lads who had come from Croatoan with Iosco and the other whites. They came to Virginia, and took her by the arm to lead her away, but Cleopatra sprang up suddenly and forced herself between them, and as she threw her arms around Virginia she cried, "Go away! who said to touch Owaissa? Nantiquas shall punish who comes near her."

One of the men replied, "Werowance Powhatan says, 'Bind every pale-face, and bring each one for the evil of him they call Barnes.'"

"I am not afraid to go to your father, the Werowance Powhatan," Virginia said calmly. "I will go with you," They led her away, and she found herself before the great chief with Beth, Patience, Gray, and Barnes, and all the other whites who had come from Croatoan.

Barnes stood tightly bound, while in front of him lay the body of an Indian whom he had killed. They had disagreed about something; and Barnes, having just heard about the ships from England, felt he was soon to be released, and ceased to be cautious. In a passion he had knocked the Indian down. As he fell, his head hit a stone, and he died immediately. Barnes had been at once dragged before the chief.

The storm broke in its fury. The prisoners had been taken to wigwams where they were well guarded. Death had been the sentence for all alike, on the morrow at break of day. Virginia was kneeling, Cleopatra clinging closely to her, wishing for Nantiquas, whom she felt sure could help them. The wind shrieked and roared outside, and the thunder rolled. Where was Iosco? Why did he not come?

CHAPTER XIV.

CHAPTER XIV.

" Every human heart is human,
  That in even savage bosom
  There are longings, yearnings, strivings,
  For the good they comprehend not,
  That the feeble hands and helpless,
  Groping blindly in the darkness,
  Touch God's right hand in that darkness,
  And are lifted up and strengthened."
                              LONGFELLOW.

WHERE was Iosco? He had followed Owaissa
in the afternoon, to tell her the news of the
English ships. He went through the forest
trail that led to the little stream just in time
to see her, Owaissa, holding Nantiquas's hand,
and looking eagerly into his face. All the
passion of his Indian nature was roused into a
hatred and jealousy of Nantiquas. He turned
quickly away, before he had been noticed, and
walked far into the woods. Was it for this that
he had given up his people, his home, his inher-
itance? For a people who cared nothing for
him. Strangely enough he found his love for
the pale-faces was really founded on his love

for one member of the race. He had never dared to hope that Owaissa would love him; she was a being too beautiful, too pure, for man to woo. Though he would never have thought of asking her to be his wife, he could not see any one else win her love. He felt that he had the first right to her. Had not he been like a brother to her, always? And he knew well that Owaissa had treated him always as a brother. He could kill Nantiquas, and then he would see. But Powhatan would no longer give them shelter. What did that matter? He would have vengeance. Iosco had thrown himself on the ground, and as he lay there, the great stillness and peace of the forest crept into his heart, and he seemed to hear Mrs. Dare's voice saying, " The dear Jesus would rather suffer all than save himself from one pain, that he might teach us the great lesson of forgiveness." " The dear Jesus," the very words brought with them a certain peace and rest. Forgive! Could he forgive Nantiquas for taking from him what he cared most for? And yet that holy Jesus forgave. A crash of thunder seemed to shake the whole forest, and the darkness crept around him, like the darkness which clouded his soul that was groping for light. Could he still live for love? For life could not be without love. Could he live for the love of that great chief, that holy Jesus? Did he want his love? How could he give his service, his life if need be? Oh, for some one to teach him as Mrs. Dare had done when he was a little child!

The storm beat fiercely against him as he rose and forced his way through the tangle of the forest. But a peace he could not describe had crept into his heart. He must be near Owaissa. To-morrow that white father might come and carry her away. He loved her, and would be near her while he might. He was tramping on, crushing everything before him like the strong man Kwasina, when a voice called to him softly. He listened. It said, " Nantiquas, is it you? "

He knew the voice. It was Cleopatra's, and it sounded full of trouble. " Is Cleopatra in sorrow? " he asked, going in the direction of the sound.

" O Nantiquas," she said, not recognizing the voice, "O Nantiquas, Owaissa is in great trouble. She is to die when the day comes, with all the pale-faces ; for Barnes, the red white man, did take the life of Nanogh, and our father says all the whites shall die."

She knew it was not Nantiquas's hand that clasped hers, and she drew back half afraid, till she heard Iosco's familiar voice.

"Owaissa is in trouble, to die! The great Werowance Powhatan would never take her life, even now as the white man is coming."

Then Cleopatra told Iosco the whole story; how, while Ramapo was telling what he had seen of the white men, the medicine-men's chant came to them; of the dreadful sentence, and how she had only now left Owaissa to watch for Nantiquas, who had gone away in his canoe in the afternoon, and had not come back. "If he would only come back," she said, "I am sure he could do something."

Iosco said, "Cleopatra must stay no longer, lest her sad tears and the rain be too much, and she die. Could she not speak to the great Werowance, and ask the life of Owaissa? He must grant what his sweet daughter wishes." Cleopatra stood up, and Iosco led her. But she said sadly, "The great Powhatan is very angry. He would never spare a captive for a child's wish, Iosco."

Suddenly Iosco loosened and drew off his large, rich wampum belt. "Will Cleopatra take this with her petition? It is the charmed belt of Manteo, my father. I prize it, but know the mighty Powhatan's eye often rests on it. He will grant the prayer of Cleopatra, if she carries the charmed belt of the far-journeyed Werowance Manteo."

She took the wampum from Iosco, and having reached her wigwam they parted, she to sleep on her tussan of stretched skins, and Iosco to find the wigwam where Owaissa slept. He would lie, but not sleep, on the wet ground outside.

The morning dawned, dull and rainy. The loving Cleopatra held the wampum belt and watched for her father to eat his food. Virginia, too, had wakened early. She thought herself deserted by Iosco, and to her surprise that thought brought more pain than the thought of her probable death, which would undoubtedly be a torturing, painful one. She little knew that Iosco had been watching by her all the night, and was even now looking sadly at her through the openings in the logs, of which the wigwam was made. He marvelled how she could kneel so calmly, her sad face more beautiful than anything he had ever seen. If Cleopatra were not successful, she would soon be led to death. He would die first, before she should suffer.

But she should not be disturbed by him in these solemn hours.

A joyous cry made Virginia look up; Iosco, too, from his post could see the lithe figure of Cleopatra as she bounded into the wigwam and threw her arms about Virginia, crying, "The beautiful Owaissa shall not die this day! The good Powhatan says that she shall fly all day and make his little daughter merry; she shall be merry at his great feast to-day, and before night comes Nantiquas will come. He will save the sweet Owaissa." •

Viginia rose, still holding the little girl in her arms, and said, "I will try to make my dear Cleopatra happy to-day, even if it be my last one she shall be merry. If Nantiquas does not come, and if he has not the power you think he has, when does Werowance say I shall die?"

Cleopatra covered her face with her brown hands to hide her tears, but she could not keep back the sobs, as she replied, "Cleopatra's father, the Werowance Powhatan, says the pretty Owaissa shall fly to-day with his child, and not die until the sun goes down and the moon comes out and the sun shines again, but when it hangs on the great pine, the Owaissa and six

of her tribe, who shall live till then, shall die
before Powhatan."

Iosco could see Owaissa comforting the child.
He heard her say, "There are other things
more cruel than death, Cleopatra, when one's
heart dies. But we will love each other to the
end, whenever it may be."

He saw her kiss the child, who clung to her,
and heard her say, "We will remember that God
knows our trouble. If he will that I should
live, he can save me even from a great Werowance like Powhatan. And if not, he will help
me to be brave."

Iosco stood quietly with unmoved face, showing nothing of the struggle and pain in his
heart.

That day there was a dreadful massacre of
nearly all the whites. They were slain before
Powhatan and his courtiers. As they were led
out, Beth Harvey caught Virginia's arm as she
passed the wigwam where Virginia stood, trying to say something encouraging to each one
as they passed. "Come, oh, come with me,
Virginia!" she cried, "stay with me to the
end." It was the old childhood name, and poor
Beth's face was so full of agony that Virginia
could not have refused her anything, so she

took her hand and went with her, and stayed with her, and kept her courage up as she had done all through her life. She stood bravely by Beth, never flinching at the dreadful sights. She did not know that Nantiquas and Iosco stood looking at her with wonder and admiration, as she held poor Beth's trembling hand, and bent all her energy to keep the little spark of courage bright.

"Dear Beth, you will be brave. It will only be a moment of pain, and then you will be beyond all pain, with your mother and with mine. But O Beth, you will know all that we have longed to know about the dear Saviour who died for us.

.   .   .   .

All was over. Beth no longer needed human aid. A slight figure, with halo of golden curls, tottered and fell. But before it touched the earth, it was caught and carried away. Under the great pine, Virginia lay motionless, while two Indian princes bent over her, doing all in their power to bring back a sign of life, and a child knelt by, crying.

Life came back; the weary brain began slowly to awake. The great blue eyes opened. She tried to smile; but that awful scene came be-

fore her,— Barnes, Gray, Smith, even Beth,
all that she had called her people, lying dead
about her. She closed her eyes; but soon she
opened them again, and found that she was
lying on the low rush tussan in the wigwam.
Nantiquas was standing, looking down at her.
At first she thought he was her father, and
stretched her hand out to him; he caught it, and
knelt down by her.

"Is it you, Nantiquas?" she said. "I forgot that you had come back."

He bent low over her as he said, "Nantiquas
is here: the Puk-weedjie hurried him back to
save the life of the sweet Owaissa."

"Save me from what? Oh, I forgot. But
how can you save me? Will Powhatan listen
to you, Nantiquas?"

She said it half dreamily, as if she didn't care.

Iosco had been lying close outside, and heard
her last words, and Nantiquas's reply, which
made him clinch his hands: —

"Powhatan will not hurt Nantiquas's wife.
To save Owaissa, she will be Nantiquas's wife,
and love him."

The voice was clear and decided, that
answered: —

"O Nantiquas, you are so good to want to

save me, but I could not be saved that way; I
could never be your wife, Nantiquas. I would
do anything else in the world that I could for
you."

After a long silence, Nantiquas replied,
" Then Owaissa will sooner die than be the wife
of Nantiquas? He cannot save her."

" No, Nantiquas," she said firmly and clearly;
"no; I can never be your wife."

He said not a word, but passed out of the
wigwam into the twilight. Cleopatra tried to
coax Virginia to eat. Iosco lay concealed at
the back of the wigwam, and wondered why
Owaissa had refused Nantiquas, till the darkness crept up and the moon rose, and the stars
came out to keep their mother moon company.
The hours slipped by, those last hours, as it
seemed, of Owaissa's life. Iosco asked himself
over and over again, should he go to her or not?

CHAPTER XV.

CHAPTER XV.

"No answer comes through the ceaseless whirl
    Of the hurrying ages tossed,
   And the New World's first little English girl
    Is still a little girl lost."

E. H. NASON.

IT was nearly the middle hour, when the darkness is thickest, that a low voice said, at the entrance of the wigwam, " Will Owaissa come? Be quick, and move like a young fawn, without noise!"

It was a very low call for Iosco to hear, but it reached him. In a moment he stood before the wigwam by Nantiquas, who only said, " We shall carry Owaissa, and Iosco must go with her. Will he go?"

The reply was prompt:—

" He will go anywhere that Owaissa will be safe; but where will that be?"

" Ask nothing now. Can you carry her?"

Iosco lifted Owaissa tenderly, as if she had been a baby, and the three passed into the darkness and silence of the forest night.

183

Nantiquas led them first behind the wigwam, where there were bushes and undergrowth to hide them. Then he turned into a trail unknown to Iosco. On, on, they went. Not a word was said. Owaissa felt that Iosco was carrying her, and she cared for nothing else. Iosco knew that he had his darling close to his heart, and that she had refused life at the price of being the wife of the bravest prince of the mightiest tribe.

Suddenly Nantiquas stopped, and said : —

" Ramapo stands yonder by the fallen willow; he loves Owaissa, and will let her pass. Iosco shall say he carries Owaissa to the great Werowance Eyonols on the Chanock flu. Say that she goes to hide at Ritanoe, in the mines of Mattasin. We meet beyond."

Iosco went on as Nantiquas said, and met Ramapo, who let him pass. But no sooner had he done it than his loyal heart repented, and he called to Iosco to return. But Iosco only ran on the more quickly. He was wondering what he should do to protect Owaissa, when he heard Nantiquas say, " Turn under the lindens to the right, quickly!" And he turned just in time to escape an arrow that Ramapo had sent after him.

Nantiquas led on in a different direction. The trail was very narrow and rough. Yet Iosco wished they might go on all night, that he might hold his prize so close.

After walking for several hours, Nantiquas stopped suddenly, and turned, saying, "The river lies just beyond. By it there is a camp, which fears not being seen, for the fire burns. The clever Powhatan has not had time to have his fire burning as bright as a harvest sun, since we started. If they are his men we shall be taken. First, Nantiquas would speak to Owaissa. He did journey to the pale-faces' camp, and lie watching and listening, but no word that Owaissa spoke came to his ears. He did see one like a spirit, so white was his face. He lays his hands together, and puts his knees on the ground, looks up and speaks, and while he does, Nantiquas seizes and carries him off in the woods. He has not the strength of a kid, but his eyes are like those of a young deer, so brown and soft. Nantiquas says to the pale-face, 'Virginia.' He nods his head and laughs, as if he knows what that is. Then Nantiquas says, 'White,' and he puts his hands to his face and laughs more. Nantiquas says, 'Dare,' and he puts one hand on the other, and looks up as

if he would say he feared the Indian not. He
would understand no more. So Nantiquas
leaves him to go back to his camp. While Nantiquas listened to the white camp men, he heard
many speak to one, the chief. But they do not
say 'White,' they say 'New-port.' One other
is 'Smi-th,' and many more such. But none
with the words of Owaissa."

Owaissa stood by Nantiquas while he spoke.
She laid her hand on his arm as she said,
" Then they have forgotten me, my own people.
But you, Nantiquas, you have been so kind, so
very good to me. I shall always love you as I
would have loved my brother. I will pray for
you always."

"Is it the prayer that makes Owaissa so
brave ? " he asked very gently.

" Yes, Nantiquas," she replied. " It is the
Great Spirit who makes us able to meet death.
Some day you will know all about him. I am
sure you will."

Nantiquas took Virginia's little hand and
pressed it one moment. Then they stepped
forward cautiously toward the river and the
light. So softly did they move, they would
surely not have been heard or discovered but
for Virginia, who, as she came nearer the fire,

gave a great cry, and sprang forward. Two figures were lying by the fire on the ground, and one was a white man.

It was an English voice that replied to Virginia's cry, " Who comes this way? "

Virginia had sprung from her two companions, and was standing in the firelight before they could stop her. She spoke in her own tongue. They could not tell what she said, but they saw the two figures, who seemed to be alone by the camp fire, draw close to her.

" Ranteo! " exclaimed Iosco. " It is old Ranteo! " and he went forward.

When the old Indian saw Iosco, he caught his hand, crying, " The people of Manteo do groan for Iosco. They offer sacrifices every day for his return. But he comes not. Old Ranteo comes far to find him and fetch him back. The brave Christian Werowance, Iosco! "

It was Owaissa who answered, turning from the stranger with whom she had been earnestly talking, " Do they really want Iosco back at Croatoan? I knew they would, some day. I am so glad, dear Iosco. "

Nantiquas and the stranger to whom Virginia had been speaking looked at each other in surprise for a moment, then they began talking by signs. Nantiquas turned to the others, and laughed as he said, " The poor pale-face could not get to his camp. He was but an arrow's fling from it."

Ranteo laughed too, as he answered, " The poor nemarough wandered like a lost deer back and forth, and was full of fear. He would speak with me, but he could not, and for the great Werowance Manteo's love, who did good to all such, Ranteo gave the stranger half his fire and half his food, and would bring him to Iosco."

Nantiquas interrupted, " The Owaissa is not safe on Powhatan's land. The boys and men wait yonder. You must go on. You must go to Croatoan. Is it not so, Iosco?"

" But how about the Werowance at Ritanoe? Must we not go there, Nantiquas?" Virginia asked.

Nantiquas laughed. " Owaissa would not have come by this trail had she been journeying to Ritanoe. Powhatan's braves have that trail to-night. Owaissa was on her way to her own people, to the camp of the pale-faces, but it is safer for her on the way to Croatoan. There she can join her people without danger from Powhatan."

A slight noise in the darkness startled them.

Iosco drew a deerskin over the fire and stepped on it till the light was gone. Nantiquas led the way, and they followed; they had gone only a short distance when they came to the men and boys, all that was left of the Roanoke colony, seven souls. Two small skiffs were waiting, a moment more and all was ready.

Owaissa clasped Nantiquas's hand. " You have been very good, dear Nantiquas. You will come to us some day, won't you?" Her voice faltered, and she sobbed as she had not done in all the scenes of pain or danger. " He has been so good; he has saved us all," she said, turning to the Englishman, who, raising his hand, gave his blessing to the young Indian prince.

One more grasp of Owaissa's hand, then the skiffs were moving down the Youghianund flu, leaving Nantiquas alone on the shore. The first rays of the sun glistened on the waving hair in the boat, and on a little silky curl in the Indian's brown hand, as he caressed it tenderly. The mists cleared away, and a faint gleam of color tinged the sky like the reflection of a rainbow. He saw it, and muttered to himself, as the skiffs passed out of sight, " Nantiquas will never tell your secret to the whites, Iosco, lest they carry her off from you." And then looking towards the bright bow of color, he added, " True, there are many flowers do die on earth."

Powhatan had condemned all the whites to die because he was afraid they might tell the secrets of his people to the white tribe who had now settled near his own lands. If they knew all, they would be dangerous enemies. So Nantiquas had sent word to Iosco not to let any of the whites attempt to go to Jamestown, for there were spies watching for them all the way, with orders to capture them. A reward was offered for every white scalp from Croatoan or Ritanoe, or wherever the seven whites had escaped to.

The old places were slowly coming nearer and nearer, and the great throb of happiness that leaps into one's heart as he is coming home, filled Virginia's heart with thankfulness and love.

" O Iosco, I am so glad I did not go right to my own people ; I would never have seen Croatoan again. I am sure there is not another place in the whole world so beautiful. I love it, every spot of its ground. Are you glad we are all to be together again for a while ? "

" Iosco is glad, oh, yes, very glad. Did Owaissa's father come in the big canoes ? What tidings brings the white man of her people?" he asked very earnestly.

Virginia was standing in the end of the skiff, that she might catch the first glimpse of the dear familiar place. She put her hand on Iosco's shoulder to steady herself, and looking sadly down into his dark eyes, she said, " O Iosco, do you know I have almost forgotten my people's language: many things the white man says to me I cannot understand. But this I do know; he says my grandfather and my father came with the big canoes to find us, long, long ago, and they found only the empty place at Roanoke and the word 'Croatoan;' but when they would find Croatoan, the storm caught up their canoes and carried them away. Even now this Chief Newport is speaking for us, and will be glad when he knows what you have done, and will give you many things."

" Will the pale-face take Owaissa to her people soon?" Iosco asked.

" Whenever you send some one with us. We could not go alone; but do not let us hurry. Let us see you back at the old place, and this white face can teach your people and all of us about the Great Spirit, the dear Jesus. Mistress Wilkins said this land needed such as he is to hallow it — a priest." Virginia said the last word reverently.

"The pale face is good. The light of the Great Spirit is in his eyes. He shall stay as long as he will, and teach the people as Manteo would have wished; and surely Owaissa will never hurry from the people who love her," Iosco replied.

"Do you know, Iosco," she said with a wistful look, "do you know I almost dread going to my people now. If I have forgotten even their language, which I once knew so well, how much less shall I know their ways and lives, which I have never learned; they will not understand me and my ways, they will laugh at me. Your people are really my people, for I know and love them."

As Iosco sprang from the little boat, upon his own land, he thought he had never felt so happy before; and when he turned and helped the Englishman on the shore, giving him a welcome after the manner of his people, Virginia wondered if the coming back had brought such joy into his face; she had not seen the pain that the leaving of it must have caused.

The priest bared his head, and raising his hand blessed the land and the people; then the

little company moved up the hill. There were
the great fields of tobacco with their long leaves
shining in the sunlight; and there were the
fields of corn where the women must have lately
been working, but now there was not a sign of
woman or child. Virginia was anxious to see
the people; and she hurried on before the others,
and ran swiftly over the grass, which was dotted
with daisies. She soon reached the council
house, which was like a great arbor, and hearing
voices she stopped and looked in.

It was, indeed, a weird, almost unearthly sight
that met her gaze. In the centre a great fire
burned; around it on the ground a circle was
formed of grains of corn; outside of this a
larger circle formed of meal. Six men, painted
red and black, with white circles painted about
their eyes, followed; another, painted like themselves, only a little more gaudily, wore on his
head a sort of crescent made of weasel-skins
stuffed with dried moss, the tails tied together
at the top with a knot of bright feathers, while
the skins fell about his face and neck; a great
green snake was coiled around his throat, the
tail flapping about on his back. The creature, who was in fact the chief medicine-man,
was a frightful object, as he danced before the

fire uttering unearthly yells. The people had assembled in the arbor, bringing with them offerings of every imaginable description for sacrifice.

The purpose of this worship was to entreat the Great Spirit to send Iosco back: they did not know how to offer the Christian sacrifice, yet they felt that their prayers must be accompanied by some proof of their earnestness ; so they used the old form of heathen worship, the only thing they had known till Manteo went to England and came back a Christian ; but even then there had been no one to teach them its blessed worship. From Manteo and Mrs. Dare they had only gained a glimmering of its first principles, which they, poor heathen people as they were, had eagerly grasped. The people inside were so intent on their worship that they did not notice Virginia, as she stood in the vine-covered doorway, or the others who soon joined her.

To Martin Atherton, the English priest, as he gazed in at the wild, weird scene, it seemed like the very entrance of hell, and that hideous figure, the chief medicine-man, looked not unlike the evil one himself, as he danced and yelled, followed closely by the others. Then all the people sent forth a groan, and the chief medicine-man threw many of the offerings the people had brought into the fire, which caused a great crackling and spluttering. The groans of the people rose dolefully, and the wild yell of the medicine-man completed the frightful scene.

When Iosco passed from the little group outside, and stood in the firelight before his people, they thought he had come out of the fire, and waited one moment to see if he would vanish into it again. As he did not, they pressed their hands to their hearts and yelled for joy, till the very rocks seemed to tremble.

At a sign from Iosco his people were silent. He spoke to them of his father, and of his Christian faith; of the whites, and how Powhatan had killed most of them; of the canoes now in the river; of how he had heard they had wanted him, and he had come. Now did they wish him to remain? With a great cry they called him their chief, while the medicine-men strewed corn before him, as a sign that all should be his, and poor old Adwa, the squaw who had nursed him, ran to the fire, and would have thrown herself in as a thank-offering had not Iosco caught her and pointed to Virginia, who still stood in the doorway. She ran to her, and held the head of soft wavy hair to her breast as tenderly as any mother would have done.

Martin Atherton looked on in amazement, at the squaws gathered about Virginia, and showed how tenderly they loved her. He could see that she loved them, and for each she seemed to have a few kind words. The children seemed to rain down, more than a dozen having gathered around her in a minute. As he watched her caress them lovingly, and saw her pick up one brown little boy, who was scarcely more than a papoose, and hold him close to her heart, he wondered if she could ever be happy in a conventional English life, and what the drawing-room would say and think of this forest maiden.

CHAPTER XVI.

CHAPTER XVI.

"Life has two ecstatic moments, one when the spirit catches sight of truth, the other when it recognizes a kindred spirit. Perhaps it is only in the land of truth that spirits can discern each other ; as it is when they are helping each other on that they may best hope to arrive there." — EDNA LYALL.

IT was the first of the Indian seasons, "the fall of the leaf." Croatoan was glorious with its colored leaves and late flowers. Weeks had slipped by since the escape from Werowocomoca. Iosco had been welcomed by his people ; so had Owaissa. The other whites, the best of the colonists who had gone to Powhatan, and thoroughly frightened by all that had happened there, were looked upon with suspicion for a long time. But the new-comer, the pale Englishman, made friends with all. He was only waiting for an opportunity to return to Jamestown. He was a priest of the church, who had worn himself out with work among the miners in England. He was broken in health, and the doctor in London had ordered a sea-voyage. Just as the colony were starting from Blackwall, Captain Newport persuaded him to go with them, promising to bring him back to his work as soon as he was strong again. So he had gone; but the name of Martin Atherton was not added to the list, though he went across to the New World. Perhaps he was sent in answer to the prayers of a maiden.

Through the long months that passed, as the summer slipped away and the autumn took its place, the prayers of Mrs. Dare, Virginia, and those few faithful souls, were answered. The poor Indians, who had had glimmerings of a higher life, through Manteo, their dearly loved chief, now listened eagerly to the message of the church, as Martin Atherton told it in a simple, direct way, while they sat in a circle on the ground about him, sometimes with great reverence kissing the sacred Book from which the holy teachings came.

Twice a day the sound of prayer and praise went up from the little congregation. Virginia had taught him the language of the people. He told her that the father she so much yearned for had not come, and he taught her about the dear Lord and his church.

Poor Iosco was in trouble again. He had never spoken of his love to Virginia, and she did all in her power to conceal her love from him. Of course he did not dream of such a possibility as her caring for him. But he watched day by day, and counted every moment she spent with Martin Atherton. Soon he would go to the white people, and then he supposed Owaissa would go too.

All Saints' Day dawned clear and bright. It was to be a great day at Croatoan, but how eventful none of them knew. It was time for the great service to begin. Virginia's face was radiant with happiness, her fair hair falling loosely over her mantle of turkey feathers.

" She might be the Queen of Sheba," thought Martin Atherton, as he came a little way behind her. " Her dignity and simplicity are perfect. Surely no one could doubt the grace of baptism who knows a soul like that, with its desire for knowledge growing stronger among heathen surroundings ; a life of praise and worship, though she does not know it. It was she that converted these heathen, not I."

He watched her as she knelt, then kneeling himself, his heart rose in earnest thanksgiving for what he had been permitted to do, and a prayer that his little Indian congregation might ever be guided aright.

The two figures were kneeling when Iosco joined them, followed by a number of his warriors, among them Ranteo, his honest face fairly glowing with happiness. He thought of the day when Manteo had been baptized in the little chapel at Roanoke. Only then he had held an ignorant reverence for the holy mystery that he was now to receive himself, with a clear knowledge of its grace and power.

The simple service began, the dear prayers that we all know and love, a simple hymn, and then the holy baptismal service. First Iosco knelt, and then a long line of Indians, all kneeling in turn reverently before the priest, were baptized from a little spring that trickled through mossy rocks.

It was a strange scene. The chapel formed of a little clearing in the forest, its walls the forest trees, its roof the arching branches, its spire a tall poplar-tree reaching towards heaven, its altar a rough rock. The open book from which the prayers were read lay on the stump of a tree: the birds joined in the hymns of praise, and the deep sigh of the wind in the forest was the organ.

The holy sign had been made on each brow, and they were henceforth no longer heathen, but soldiers of the great King. Martin Atherton stood before his little congregation and spoke to them. He did not preach on systematic theology, or discuss the question whether St. Paul's garment was his cloak or a vestment ; he spoke as a great soul bringing a great message. He tried to show his hearers the power of the gospel in the past and in the present. He told it simply, but with an eloquence that held every one. His clear voice rang through the forest, with the last words, " Then shall the righteous shine forth as the sun in the kingdom of their Father." A great silence crept over the little congregation as the preacher raised his hand for the invocation, but not a sound came. He raised his eyes, and fell backwards without a word. He lay motionless by the rude altar. Loving hands raised his head and laid it on Virginia's knee. For a moment the people gathered silently around the unconscious form, then drew away, that they might not keep the reviving air from him, allowing Virginia and Iosco to do what they could, only following their directions. At last the dark eyes opened and saw Virginia's beautiful face filled with sorrow and anxiety.

"Dear child," he said, as he had often spoken before, "please raise my head a little more. This may pass, and I may be better soon; don't be anxious. If not "— he only smiled and did not finish.

"Oh, you must not die!" Virginia cried; "we need you; so does God's work in this sad world."

"God does not need us, dear child: it is we that need him. You will always be true and faithful to your holy vows, and when the day comes for you to go to England and to your people, you will have teachers sent to these people who are yours by adoption."

Somehow the thought of going to England added to Virginia's pain at that moment, and she drew closer to Iosco as the speaker fell into a state of unconsciousness. Looking up into Iosco's face, she read something new that she had never seen there before. He had longed for the Christian faith; he had wished for his baptism; he had believed all that Martin Atherton had taught. The service that morning had changed him. Those blessed drops "had worked wonder there, earth's chambers never knew." The right of a new birth, the perfect faith of the man before him, had given Iosco something he could not explain, but he knew and felt that the dear Lord was very near, and the knowledge of that perfect love filling his heart, his whole life, brought a peace which the world could never take away. It made him worthy of human love, and yet it made him feel it was quite possible to live without it. When we can say truthfully in our hearts, "Thy will be done," God sends us often so great a blessing that it almost frightens us as we receive it.

The little congregation had moved away. Hours slipped by. Only Virginia and Iosco watched by their friend, who still lay as if dead, with only the slight, uneven fluttering of his heart to show that there was yet life in the worn-out body.

Virginia looked up at Iosco, and speaking softly, said, "If he really gets better, you ought to send him to his people, that he may see them before he dies."

"The blessed priest shall be carried before the sunrise and laid among his people if he lives. Iosco's warriors shall keep him from harm by Powhatan. The Owaissa can then go without fear to her people, and be happy," he replied.

"To-morrow, Iosco? So soon? O Iosco" — Virginia faltered. Looking down suddenly into her upturned face he read her great love. The two looked into each other's eyes long and earnestly, and each read the other's heart. Iosco knelt, putting his arm around her, and whispered, "Owaissa, my Owaissa!" He kissed her forehead again and again; and she laid her head on his breast and clung to him as she said, "I will never, never go, Iosco. Your people shall be my people. We shall be all to each other now."

"My Owaissa will be all to Iosco forever." When one soul which truly loves looks deep into another and reads there the answering love he has longed for, he knows what a great treasure he has better than any one could tell him; and to both souls comes the sense that they are no longer separate beings, but one in each other. A golden light has spread over the world, which, thank God, nothing earthly has the power to destroy.

Two dark eyes had opened and were watching them. Iosco was the first to notice that their friend had roused; and, bending over him, he asked if he wished to be taken to his own people. The holy priest said with a gentle smile, "There will not be time; I shall die among these people; they are dear to me."

At his suggestion, the people were summoned.

He was raised and supported, and performed the last act of ministry on earth.

A Christian wedding was a strange sight to these poor people. It was over; Owaissa and Iosco sat together, and watched by their friend till the sun set, when his soul passed in the glory of the golden sky to the perfect glory and brightness of the people of God.

The story of the life of the first American child has never been recorded in history; but that life, we know, was not wasted.

Who can tell what a pure, brave life may do? Lived in humble station in this nineteenth century, or in the wild forest three hundred years ago, as was VIRGINIA DARE'S!

www.ingramcontent.com/pod-product-compliance
Lightning Source LLC
Chambersburg PA
CBHW020617030726
47497CB00007B/2279